The Proud Mr Peverill

By the same author

TENDER TRAP
ISLAND FOR FIONA
ROMANCE IN RAVENDALE
HAUNTED BY SANDRA
HEARTBREAK AT HAVERSHAM
WAITING FOR MATT
MISTRESS OF CALVERLEY
A DISGRACEFUL DECEIT
A WAYWARD MISS
THE SCHEMING MR CLEEVE
AN OUTRAGEOUS MASQUERADE
THE HANDSOME SMUGGLER
THE ENIGMATIC MR FARRAR

The Proud Mr Peverill

Gillian Kaye

ROBERT HALE · LONDON

© Gillian Kaye 2002
First published in Great Britain 2002

ISBN 0 7090 7096 9

Robert Hale Limited
Clerkenwell House
Clerkenwell Green
London EC1R 0HT

The right of Gillian Kaye to be identified as
author of this work has been asserted by her
in accordance with the Copyright, Design and
Patents Act 1988.

2 4 6 8 10 9 7 5 3 1

Typeset in 11/16pt Garamond
Derek Doyle & Associates, Liverpool.
Printed in Great Britain by
St Edmundsbury Press Ltd, Bury St Edmunds, Suffolk.
Bound by Woolnough Bookbinders Ltd

To Betty, with love

ONE

Anna stared at her mother in astonishment. 'Mama, it cannnot be true. You must be mistaken.'

Mrs Elizabeth Starkie, widow of the late Thomas Starkie of Ponderfields in the village of West Wilton near Bath, looked at her daughter as though to censure her for her remark; then she changed her mind and looked back at the letter she was holding in her hand.

The letter had just been delivered to the house and the maid had hurried into the drawing-room for the money. For this was 1813, and the charge for postage was paid by the recipient of the mail, not by the sender.

Breakfast was over and the young Starkie girls had gone up to the schoolroom. Mrs Starkie and her eldest daughter, Anna, were sitting in the drawing-room to talk over the events of the day ahead of them. Mrs Starkie would then go and discuss the meals with cook.

This routine caused no little amusement to Anna as, in their impoverished state, one day was much like another and their dinners usually consisted of a cheap piece of mutton which was served cold or hashed for several days after its first airing.

Mrs Starkie, left a widow two years before, and with four girls to bring up was usually a timid creature though a loving mother. She clutched the letter just delivered to her and tried to speak firmly to Anna.

'Please will you listen again, Anna, I insist upon it. And I am not in the habit of being mistaken over a letter from a lawyer which is written in plain English.'

Anna, tall and fair, but with no claim to beauty except in the soft greyness of her eyes, recognized her mama's rare excursion into authority and sat obediently attentive. 'Very well, Mama,' she murmured.

'The letter is from your godmother's lawyer, Mr Bainbridge. We know that it is a month since your godmother died and I cannot think what has caused the delay in writing to us. As you have always known, Joan Hamlyn was a very dear friend of my schooldays. We both attended Miss Wykeham's establishment for young ladies in Knightsbridge. She was the Lady Joan Hamlyn, eldest daughter of the Earl of Plucknett and I was plain Elizabeth Southwell; but it made no difference, we were bosom bows right until the time of my marriage to your dear father and my removal to Bath.'

Anna was becoming impatient. 'But I know all this, Mama; what has it to do with the contents of the lawyer's letter, which I cannot believe for one moment?'

'I am trying to explain, dear. Joan was the eldest of five girls and all her sisters married well; Joan remained a spinster until the day she died. Now this is what we did not know until this very moment. Her father, the earl, had no sons and when he died, his younger brother inherited the title and the estate – well, we did know that for Joan went on living at Lambley Hall with her uncle and his family, she told me so in her letters, but – and this is what is important – the bulk of her father's fortune was left to Joan....'

Anna was trying to concentrate on her mother's explanation. 'But, Mama, what about her poor uncle? He must have needed the money for his own family,' she interrupted.

'No, you are wrong. It seems that her uncle had married a considerable heiress and in any case, he would have had the income from the Lambley Park estate. The lawyer explains all this and then stipulates that a legacy of ten thousand pounds is bequeathed to Lady Joan's god-daughter, Miss Anna Starkie, and he says he would be grateful if Miss Starkie would visit him in his London office where he would await her instructions. There, I have told you exactly what he has said.'

Mrs Starkie eyed her daughter, expecting a triumphant expression, but all she could discern was a look of numbed disbelief. 'Well, Anna?' she said impatiently, but she received no reply. 'You do realize that ten thousand pounds invested in the funds will give you a handsome income and that you will become a very rich and sought after young lady.'

Anna indeed felt numbed just as her mother had perceived. Never a wealthy family, since Mr Starkie's death, they had struggled on an income of less than £600 a year. True, they had been able to keep the carriage and George-Coachman, and Miss Swinburne the governess had been retained; but there had been no money to spare for Anna's come-out or a season in Bath where, if not a beauty, her fine fair curls and pleasing manner would have been sure to attract a good offer.

Anna stood up and faced her mother across the fireplace. Even though she had to endure the strictest economies, Mrs Starkie insisted on a fire in the drawing-room on these cool mornings of early May. 'Mama, I cannot immediately conceive the importance of this news; that it will make a difference to our circumstances, I readily understand, but you cannot expect me to imagine what it means to have a sudden fortune thrust upon one.' She felt that she was speaking stiffly, but she was quite overwhelmed and needed the time to think. 'I can hardly remember my godmother even though she visited on one occasion when I was small. But she always kindly remembered me on my birthday....'

'And you always wrote a pretty reply, my dear,' she was reminded by her mother.

Anna nodded. 'Yes, but pretty replies do not deserve a fortune of ten thousand pounds. And what about all her nephews and nieces? There must be many of them if my godmother had four sisters.'

'All well provided for, she told me so many times for I know she was fond of them. And now we can provide for you, Anna. We can go to London to see the lawyer and sign the papers – just you and me, not the children. And we will visit the best mantua-maker and milliner in town and when we return, we will make plans for your come-out as soon as the season starts.'

But Anna protested strongly. 'No, Mama, you are going too fast for me. I do not wish my fortune to be known in the neighbourhood, for I would have every gazetted fortune-hunter applying for my hand. If I marry, I want it to be for myself and not for my fortune ... no, Mama, it is no use objecting. You go and speak to cook as you always do at this time and I will go for a walk to think things over. It is a fine morning and will give me a chance to reflect. And please say nothing about this morning's letter; not even to the girls.'

Mrs Starkie also stood up; she was not as tall as Anna, but was by no means frail in spite of her forty-five years and the sorrow of losing a beloved husband. And she knew Anna in this mood, for Anna at twenty years of age had been taking the guiding strings of the household from the time of her father's death and her eighteenth birthday.

'Yes, dear, a walk will do you good. We will talk again and make our plans when you return. I promise you that I will say nothing of your news to Miss Swinburne, or cook, or anyone.' And she left the room. Anna knew that it would be diffcult for her mother not to speak of her good fortune, but that she would keep her word.

Anna ran upstairs to fetch her pelisse and bonnet; it was not a difficult choice as she possessed just the one deep-blue pelisse of a strong calico which served her summer and winter alike. She had worn it for several years without complaint and had ceased to remember how well it became her grey eyes and fair curls.

Ponderfields had been an extensive estate in West Wilton, a few miles to the south of Bath and not far from the village of Englishcombe. When Mr Starkie had died, the land had been sold off to provide a modest income for his remaining family; it had been to Mr and Mrs Starkie's sorrow that no son survived to succeed to the estate. Anna was their first born and then had come two weakly little boys who had died in their early years; they were succeeded by three girls, Felicity, Selina and Jane, all under fourteen years of age and being taught by the worthy Miss Swinburne.

With her thoughts in chaos, that morning Anna chose to walk down their short front garden and through the gate into fields which were part of the neighbouring Hatherley Park estate. Anna could hardly remember a time when there had been a family at Hatherley; the house was large and imposing and kept in order by the faithful Mr and Mrs Shapter. Mr Shapter had been the head gardener and Mrs Shapter the cook, in the old days. Now they were both elderly and cared for the building until the day came when someone would rent it. Village people would say that they thought it was owned by a distant Wiltshire family, but this was uncertain. A steward would arrive every month to collect the rents and see to any repairs on the farms.

So the woods and fields of Hatherley had been Anna's playground and she came here with her small sisters and sometimes with Miss Swinburne when the fine weather tempted them out. She also came here with Christopher – but she must put all thoughts of Christopher from her mind for the moment. Ten thousand pounds. It was a sum almost impossible to imagine; her mind was tuned to shillings and pounds, even to hundreds of pounds, but ten thousand was more than could be reckoned with except if one thought of the income that it would provide if it was sensibly invested.

And Anna rebelled. I don't want it, she thought stormily. We live frugally but we are happy. I suppose I must think of the girls. I will have it invested so that when the time comes, Felicity, Selina and Jane can have their portion and be nicely dressed and have their come-out and season in a way which would make them happy. I can buy dresses and gowns for Mama, and I suppose, for myself. Though I am quite comfortable and happy in this old blue pelisse.

Her thoughts were flitting from one thing to another but always coming back to Christopher.

Mr Christopher Boyd, soon to be the Reverend Boyd, was the son of the rector of West Wilton; he was reading for the church at Oxford and hoped to have a parish of his own before the year was out. Then he wanted to marry Anna.

He had hesitated when he had asked her to marry him for he knew that a vicar's income was not large. Anna had not refused his first offer because of this; she had refused him because she was not sure that she loved him in the way she had always romantically hoped she would love the man she was to marry.

She had known Christopher for as long as she could remember for he was just two years older than she was and the Starkie girls had grown up thinking of the rector's boys almost as brothers.

I could marry Christopher now, thought Anna as she entered the wood which lay at the edge of the Hatherley estate. It was a dense wood of oaks and elms and some magnificent beeches; it had become quite overgrown except for the broad path at its centre which Mr Shapter had always kept clear for the Starkie children. Its canopy barely let the sun through at this time of year, but here and there a glance of sunlight hit the path in what Anna thought was a magical way.

Her thoughts continued on the theme of Christopher. He was a handsome young man, slender and dark; always very proper towards her, but with an affectionate air of mischief in his manner when he was with her. In such a way, he would have treated a favourite sister. And that is the problem, thought Anna, we are as brother and sister and so comfortable together. But was it comfort alone she wanted? He had never kissed her, he had not even told her that he loved her when he made his offer of marriage, having very properly asked Mrs Starkie's permission first.

As Anna's thoughts became tumultuous at the thought of marrying for love and passion and not for propriety and convenience, she became aware of a movement at the far end of the woodland path. Immediately, she thought it must be Mr Shapter and started to hurry forward to greet him. As she drew nearer, she stopped abruptly in her tracks; for anyone less likely than the elderly and bent Mr Shapter in his leather jerkin would be hard to imagine.

In front of her, standing still and looking imperiously at her through his eyeglass, was a very tall gentleman. His dress proclaimed the gentleman if his bearing had not already informed her of it; in a dark-blue coat of superbly cut superfine, silver-embroidered grey waistcoat and with pantaloons of the same colour, he eyed her with an air which could only be described as supercilious.

Anna stayed still and lifted her head to him for she was intrigued. A gentleman, a perfect stranger, and in the grounds of Hatherley Park.

He strode towards her then and his stride was not the mince of a fop or dandy. His voice as it reached her was both haughty and suspicious.

'And might I ask, ma'am, if you are in the habit of trespassing in the grounds of Hatherley Park?'

Anna lifted her head even higher and light grey eyes clashed with those of a deeper and penetrating grey.

'I have walked this path all my life, sir.' She was surprised at the coolness of her tone for she found that her heart was thumping. 'I have never considered it to be trespassing as there has not been an owner of the park for many years, and Mr Shapter always makes us welcome. In fact, he has kept the broad walk through the wood clear for us to trespass, as you so pointedly put it.'

By this time, Anna was aware that she was talking to a gentleman who had not only good looks and striking dark hair, but who was possessed of a forceful personality. Was she about to learn who he was and what he was doing there?

She saw him stiffen and his eyeglass drop. His voice was cutting. 'I have no wish to know who you are, but in future you will kindly avoid walking in the grounds of Hatherley Park. I have taken up residence here and do not wish to be disturbed by people from the village. Good-day.'

Anna, dumbfounded by his rudeness, watched him walk away and disappear from the wood. She turned and hurried back along the walk, not knowing if she was intrigued, angry or simply curious.

What an odious man, she said the words out loud, and such proud, haughty manners. He reminds me of Mr Darcy in *Pride and Prejudice*. All the Starkies had been enthralled by the book which had been published earlier that year 'By the Author of *Sense and Sensibility*'.

And he thought me one of the village people; I might look

shabby genteel, but could he not tell that I was a lady? Is it possible that he has come to live at Hatherley Park? Just like Mr Bingley at Netherfield, except in manner, of course.

I must hurry back and tell Mama, Anna was thinking, as she reached the edge of the wood and took the field path.

'Anna, there you are.' It was Christopher and she felt so pleased to see his familiar, friendly face, his dark hair slightly unruly.

'Christopher . . . oh, I am so pleased to see you.'

And she ran across the field straight into his arms. He held her closely and she felt the comfort and reassurance she needed. She had never received an embrace from him before and she drew away shyly, with the feeling that it had been forward of her.

'No, let me hold you,' Christopher said, with a suspicion of impudence. 'I have not had my arms around you before and I like it. And why is Miss Starkie so pleased to see me? Have you met a ghost in the wood?'

The embrace was seen by the new owner of Hatherley Park; after leaving her, he had taken a walk round the wood and had come into the open just as a young gentleman had appeared at the edge of the field. Then he heard the call – though not the words – and saw the young woman he had spoken to running across the field to be taken and held closely in the gentleman's arms.

So, he said to himself, the village maiden has a lover and their tryst is probably here in the wood. She is telling him all about me and I doubt it is good tidings. A striking girl, he thought, rather shabbily dressed, yet her voice was of the gentry rather than the village. He watched as they walked across the next field into the garden of the neighbouring house which he knew to be Ponderfields; as they disapeared, he turned away to continue the survey of his estate.

Not knowing that she was being watched, Anna laughed up at Christopher. 'It was not a ghost,' she told him. 'It was a very rude gentleman. I do not know who he is but he says that he has taken Hatherley Park. And, Christopher, I thought he was like Mr Darcy in *Pride and Prejudice*. You read it, too, so you will know what I mean.'

'I do know, young lady, but I hope that you do not imagine yourself in the role of Elizabeth Bennet. You belong to me. And I came to tell you especially that indeed we have a new neighbour at Hatherley Park—'

'You know who he is?' Anna interrupted quickly.

He smiled down at her. 'I do, for he called to see Father as his first courtesy. I have not met him as you seem to have done, but I understand him to be extremely obliging.'

'Fiddle, he was rude. There is no other word for it. He did not introduce himself, and neither did he ask my name for he obviously thought I was a village girl. He accused me of trespassing, *and* he said he did not wish to be disturbed by people from the village.' She looked at him curiously. 'Did you learn his name? He must be a viscount at least.'

'No, you are wrong. He is plain Mr Philippe Peverill of Hatherley Park, and it seems he has no wife. He told Father that his cousin, Miss Thora Peverill, is to keep house for him.'

'Philippe, Philippe?' Anna murmured the name. 'Why not Philip? Philippe sounds French. There is a mystery about this proud Mr Peverill.'

Christopher laughed. 'I can see that you are set to dislike him. But tell me, Anna, why were you walking in the wood so early in the morning? You usually wait until I arrive and then we decide what to do. I am not due back in Oxford until the tenth of the month so we still have a few days to ourselves.'

'Let us walk back to the house,' Anna replied, 'and I will tell you my news. You will never believe it, Christopher. I can hardly believe it myself. You are the only person outside the family to be told. I refuse to own up to being an heiress.'

'Whatever are you talking about, Anna? You are making it sound as though you have inherited a fortune.'

Anna laughed for the first time that day. 'That is precisely what has happened. My godmother, Lady Joan Hamlyn, died last month and she has left me ten thousand pounds.'

'Goddammit, Anna, you must be bamming me.'

'No, it is true and Mama says that if it is invested in the funds, it will bring in a generous income—' She broke off as she saw his expression darken. 'What is it, you do not look pleased.'

He shook his head. 'Good Lord, Anna, surely you can see it. Everyone will think I am marrying you for your money.'

Anna stopped as they reached the next gate. 'There are two things to say to that remark. The first is that although you have made me an offer of marriage, I have yet to accept it; and the second is that no one will know of my fortune. Oh, maybe I will let it abroad that I have received a bequest from my godmother. I will be able to have a season this year and I can buy dresses for the girls, gowns for Mama. Perhaps we can eat beef or venison instead of the eternal cold mutton, we might even manage ponies for my sisters. But that is as far as it will go. I refuse to be courted for my wealth. And if I marry anyone at all, it will be you . . . no, I have *not* accepted you. I have tried to put you in the picture.'

Christopher thought he knew his Anna. She had been the close companion of his boyhood and his youth; now he wanted her by his side as his wife. He was fond of her, she came from a good family and, what was most important of all to him, she was accustomed to managing on a small income. He could not expect more than a modest stipend when he obtained a parish of his own. Now she had not only inherited a fortune, she was going to deny it.

'Anna, I don't know what your dear mother is going to say to all this. Does she know of your decision?'

'Yes, I did hint at it. I left her so that I could go and walk in the wood to think over the implications of my inheritance. Mama will agree with me as long as I have a season and leave her free from any financial worry.' She leaned against the gate and looked up at him. This was the good man she thought she would have to marry because no one else would offer for the Miss Starkie who owned only one pelisse. Maybe she would marry him and bring something more than just comfort into their lives. She found the thought sobering that morning, but she did not want the opposite. She did not want a string of mamas calling at Ponderfields seeking her fortune for their penniless sons. She did not want to enter the Upper Rooms in Bath and be pointed out as the rich Miss Starkie. She told Christopher all this and he opened the gate for her and she said as she thanked him, 'Let us go and tell Mama.'

By the time Anna had finished telling her mother that she was not going to acknowledge her inheritance, Mrs Starkie needed the vinaigrette.

'I have bred a monster,' she told Christopher, whom she loved as though he had been her own son. Anna had left the room for a few minutes. 'All the advantages that money can bring her and she is going to pretend that it is next to nothing. Do you suppose she is a nip-farthing?'

Christopher smiled at the expression on such respectable lips as Mrs Starkie's, but he spoke honestly. 'Anna is generous to a fault, but she don't want to be chased after for her money. I am left with the feeling that I should withdraw my suit. . . .'

'No, Christopher, I want you as a son. Do not desert us just when we need you most.'

'I won't do that, Mrs Starkie, for you are my second family and always have been. But if Anna can keep the size of her fortune from the tabbies, at least I won't be accused of marrying her for her money.'

Anna returned and gave her mother a kiss. 'You shall have the finest gowns which money can buy, Mama. Now you must hear the rest of our news.'

Mrs Starkie looked from one to the other. 'Whatever do you mean? Is not a fortune enough for one morning?'

Anna and Christopher laughed, and Anna told her mother of the encounter in the wood.

Then Christopher took up the tale. 'He has called to see Father and his name is Mr Philippe Peverill.'

'Peverill?' questioned Mrs Starkie with some excitement in her voice. 'A Peverill at Hatherley Park? To think of it being unoccupied all these years. I believe my father knew a Peverill in London, a notable family. And has he a wife and children? This is an extraordinary morning for news. We live such quiet, secluded lives and all this happens in one day. I must assume he will call with his card very soon for we are his nearest neighbours.'

Mr Peverill called the very next day and Mrs Starkie and Anna were invited to Hatherley for dinner the following evening; the Reverend Boyd would be there with Mrs Boyd and their two eldest boys and he would like them all to meet his cousin.

Anna watched him curiously as he talked to her mother; his expression was less severe, but was far from being either kindly or sociable. However, all this was lost on Mrs Starkie who seemed to be bewitched by his faultless manners and his exquisite waistcoat and the intricate fall of his lightly starched, pure white neck-cloth.

As he prepared to leave, he turned to Anna for the first time; she had been thinking that he had not noticed her presence, but it did not vex her. She had been amused by his easy approach to her mother.

'Miss Starkie, I feel I owe you an explanation. Would you do me the honour of walking as far as my curricle with me? I did not need the carriage to come such a short distance.'

'I would be delighted, Mr Peverill,' Anna replied smoothly, and she saw him glance at her sharply. He had not missed the note of irony in her voice.

They stood at the gate of the small front garden at Ponderfields. 'You have a charming house, Miss Starkie. I understand that your father died a little while ago and that his land was added to Hatherley Park.'

'That is correct; it was two years ago, sir.'

'My condolences, it must be hard for your mother.'

'It is my hope that I give all the support that I can.'

'Of course.' He paused and took in her appearance. In a well-worn but pretty sprig muslin, her fair curls rather loose around her shoulders and candid grey eyes looking fearlessly into his, he realized that he had been quite mistaken to have thought her a village girl. He wondered who the young man had been. 'I have yet to meet all my neighbours. I called at the Rectory and Mr Boyd agreed to bring his two eldest sons to dinner tomorrow. You know them, no doubt?'

He is curious about something, thought Anna, I will keep him guessing.

'I have known them all my life, Mr Peverill.'

'I understand that the eldest boy who is still at home – Christopher, I think his father called him – is about to enter the church.'

'Christopher wished to follow his father,' was the brief reply.

Dammit, she is holding me at bay, he thought. I believe it to have been Christopher Boyd whom she met at the wood, but she is going to say nothing; I will find out tomorrow at dinner. I wonder what it is about her that intrigues me?

'I shall meet him tomorrow, of course,' he said aloud. 'I wish to be on good terms with my neighbours. But I must repeat my warning of yesterday, Miss Starkie: please do not venture on to Hatherley land. I hope to invite friends for the shooting when the season comes and would not like there to be any accidents.'

'Of course not.'

'You are a young lady of very few words,' he observed.

'It depends with whom I am in conversation, Mr Peverill.'

A put-down, he thought. Who the deuce does Miss Starkie think she is? Two can play at that game.

'I agree with you, ma'am. With some people, one can be on easy terms, while with others there seems to be an indefinable barrier to any kind of social contact or rapport.'

'Perhaps it develops on better acquaintance,' she said evenly, and amazed herself at keeping him at a distance for so long.

'I doubt our acquaintance will improve if you are taken up with the rectory boys,' he replied with an edge.

'And who said I was "taken up with them" as you put it?'

'You implied it, ma'am.'

'Implication can be sometimes mistaken,' she returned, and began to wonder if this was the fun-loving Anna Starkie who was speaking.

He made a bow. 'Miss Starkie, we will continue our acquaintance at dinner tomorrow. I almost look forward to a further exchange of words with you.'

'Certainly, sir. I bid you good-day.'

And Anna turned and made what she hoped was a dignified return to the house. What an insufferable prig, she was saying to herself. He will soon be thinking that he owns the neighbourhood.

At three o'clock the next afternooon, the Starkie carriage set off on the brief journey to Hatherley Park, carrying Mrs Starkie and Anna in the finest dresses which their wardrobe could provide.

They were admitted to the drawing-room to be greeted by a tall and rather large lady, splendidly dressed in deep crimson satin and with a feathered head-dress.

'Mrs Starkie, Miss Starkie, I must introduce myself and extend apologies on behalf of my cousin.' Her voice boomed and Anna thought she imagined a hint of commonness which she would not have expected in a cousin of Mr Philippe Peverill.

'I am Thora Peverill, second cousin to dear Philippe and one day to be his wife. I hope I make that clear.' This was said with something of a smirk and looking directly at Anna, who could hardly repress a chuckle. She knew she was being warned off. 'My cousin has suddenly been called away on urgent business so I hope that you will not object to me playing the hostess for him. We are expecting a party from the rectory. Mrs Shapter is an excellent cook and I see no reason why Philippe's enforced absence should spoil a good dinner and an occasion for me to meet my neighbours.'

TWO

Miss Thora Peverill was eyed with some curiosity by Anna; she seemed to be an improbable future wife for the Mr Philippe Peverill whom Anna had met only on those two occasions. She admitted to herself that she knew little about him, but his pride and his dignity did not seem to fit easily with this cousin of his. For Thora Peverill soon turned out to be a gabble-monger.

'Do sit down, Mrs Starkie and Anna, if I may call you Anna. There is no need to be formal if we are to be near neighbours. And I have to get used to country ways; I can hardly comprehend dinner at four o'clock after the later hours we kept in London. Philippe has a fine London house, you know, but it has long been his wish to have a place in the country. So here we are at Hatherley Park and near to Bath as well. That I shall enjoy for I am quite the one for balls and assemblies, even though I do not dance myself. Is the waltz frowned upon in Bath? Ah, I hear the front door, it must be the party from the rectory. The Reverend and Mrs Boyd and two of their boys. I understand that the eldest boy – John, I believe – is in the Peninsula. How the war drags on, there must be an end to it soon with dear Lord Wellington in charge of things.' She turned to the door as the party was admitted and hardly paused for breath. 'Mrs Boyd, and this is Christopher? And Jeremy, of course. Do come in. You know our other guests very well, I believe. I have just been explaining to them that Philippe has been called away on business, but that need not spoil a cosy dinner for us all. And what news is there from over the channel? I hope that John keeps you informed . . . you were going to say, Mrs Boyd? I do prattle on so; indeed Philippe calls me a rattle-pate sometimes. He does so love to tease me, you know.'

Anna listened to this rigmarole in fascination; she could not reconcile it with the autocratic reserve of Miss Peverill's cousin. But she looked at the Boyds wondering if indeed there was any news from John, the eldest of the Boyd family.

In the spring of 1813, all England was longing for news from the Peninsula. Wellington's men had spent the winter on the border of Spain and Portugal and it was expected that he would push the French through Spain back to their own border.

The Boyds had, in fact, received a letter from John that very morning; he had joined as an ensign in the militia and had marched as a redcoat through Portugal, surviving the battles of both Talavera and Salamanca.

Mr Boyd looked round at the assembled company with great pleasure. 'Ma'am, I am pleased to make your acquaintance and I am sorry that Mr Peverill is not at home to hear the good news which we have received this morning. It is a letter from our son, John, and it is much to our relief as we have had no news for several months. We do know, of course, from the morning paper that the army has spent the winter on the border of Portugal and Spain. I will read the most important part to you – it was written in early April:

> *. . . as you know, it was a terrible experience for us to have to retreat across Spain. Indeed, it was humiliating and even as we reached the hills of the Portuguese frontier, the weather turned against us. For four days we had no*

rations. I have no wish to dwell on such a terrible time, but I suppose I must look on the bright side. We ran into a herd of swine and they provided hundreds of us with a good dinner. I remained well in spite of the cold and the onset of typhus and yellow fever. And we were all cheered when we had the news of Napoleon's retreat from Moscow – it seems that it was not only in Portugal that it was a hard winter. The spring is late but we march hopefully towards Burgos and Vitoria, and we are not far from the seaport of Santander so maybe this letter will reach you quickly.

My love to you and not to forget our friends at Ponderfields – are Christopher and Anna married yet? Please remember us all in your prayers.

Your loving son
John

Anna went over to Mrs Boyd and kissed her; the rector's wife was a kind and motherly figure and Anna knew that she had hopes of herself and Christopher. 'I am so pleased for you, Mrs Boyd, to have such good news. It must be comforting for John to think of us all here in West Wilton.' She turned to Christopher who was smiling at her. 'Christopher, I am sorry that we have to disappoint John, but you will give him my love when you write to him, will you not?'

'It is all splendid news,' broke in Miss Peverill. 'Do you mean that you are not going to marry Christopher, Anna dear? How very disappointing. A wedding is always such fun, especially in families as close as you are. Has Anna turned you down, Christopher? You must keep trying, you know. They say in the best circles that it is polite for the lady to refuse the first offer from a gentleman. I shall keep my eye on the two of you and see what I can do to get you together. I enjoy match-making, I must say, and I. . . .'

Anna did not hear the next words such was her astonishment at the audacity and familiarity of Miss Thora Peverill. Why, she is almost vulgar, she was thinking. However does she come to be a cousin of Mr Peverill? But she did say only a second cousin so maybe that explains it – but she is a Peverill nonetheless.

When Anna's attention returned to their hostess, she found that Miss Peverill was speaking of her cousin. Anna listened with interest – it seemed one had only to listen when in the company of Mr Philippe Peverill's relative and housekeeper. She wondered what Christopher was thinking. She dared to look at him, caught his eye and he grinned and raised his eyebrows at her. We might find out something about your new neighbour, he seemed to be telling her.

'. . . and I am very sorry that dear Philippe is not hear to receive you. He is often away and I have learned not to ask him where he has been; it would seem impolite of me. Though I do not believe that it is a ladybird who keeps him from home, in spite of him having a house in Weymouth. Oh dear, my tongue has probably shocked you speaking of a ladybird like that. I don't know the correct word, light-of-love I suppose would do. I do not like to speak of my cousin having a mistress when he has more or less promised to marry me. It was always planned in the family that we should marry for we are the same age and have the same interests . . .'

Anna nearly choked with laughter and did not look at Christopher, who, in any case, had yet to meet their new neighbour. She herself had thought Mr Peverill to be a gentleman in the prime of life, in his mid-thirties she had judged him to be but, it was evident to all that his cousin would not see her fortieth birthday again. She was certainly a handsome woman, Anna had to be honest, but there was something very unappealing about her with her loose talk and her attempts at familiarity.

In the weeks which followed, Miss Thora Peverill ingratiated herself with most of the respectable families of the neighbourhood and Mr Philippe Peverill had still not returned. Rumours about him were rife; with a name like Philippe, he must be a French spy, a house in Weymouth would give him easy access to France; he had been seen in Weymouth with a very fetching young lady who was obviously a lady of the town, she looked up at him so pertly. Then someone saw him further along the Dorset coast dressed in rough clothing, and it was rumoured that he was a smuggler and his absences were to fetch brandy from the French ports and convey it to the ready markets of London where any chance of avoiding the crippling taxes of the time was eagerly seized upon.

Anna listened to all these tales and then made her own speculations which she divulged only to Christopher. The two of them were now obliged to take their walks along the stream which flowed fast along the end of the rectory garden and towards Ponderfields. Over the years, a path had been worn along its banks and it made a pleasant summer stroll, shaded in many parts by the willow trees which dipped their branches into the water.

'Christopher,' Anna said, one warm morning in June, 'since you have been home from Oxford, have you heard of these tales of Mr Peverill which are circulating?' The young man was now an ordained priest and awaited the opportunity of hearing of a curacy or a parish which he hoped would not be too far distant.

He laughed at Anna's question. He was holding her hand, the nearest approach to intimacy which he permitted himself. 'I have heard from at least three sources that he is a French spy and one person said that he travels between London, Weymouth and Paris, though if that is so, I cannot imagine what he is doing with a large estate in Somersetshire.'

'I believe the suspicion arose because he is called *Philippe* instead of the English Philip,' Anna replied.

'That is tenuous to say the least of it. What do you think, Anna? Don't forget that you are one of the few people to have met him.'

'From my conversation with him and my observation of his character, indeed of his dress and deportment, I have decided that he is just the sort of gentleman to keep a mistress in Weymouth—'

'Anna, that is casting a slur which is not at all like you.'

'But you know that I took him in instant dislike,' she told him. 'He was so top-lofty and condescending; I just cannot imagine him tolerating his cousin's endless chat for very long; he probably takes himself off to Weymouth to the arms of his piece of muslin.'

Christopher was shocked but he knew his Anna. 'You ain't supposed to know of such things, Anna,' he protested, with an air of horror which she knew very well was pretended.

'I have not grown up with you and John for nothing, you know,' she replied with a laugh.

He sighed. 'Well, the latest story I've heard is that Miss Peverill is letting it be known that she is the possessor of a handsome fortune and that her cousin is obliged to marry her. He is a younger son and was profligate in his youth and he hasn't got a sixpence to scratch with ... no, you did not hear me say that, Anna, not fit for your ears. Can't help picking up these expressions in Oxford even if one is reading for the church.' He turned her towards him, smiling at her. 'You had better not let him know that you are possessed of a fortune; he will transfer his allegiance from Miss Thora to yourself.'

'Fudge,' she retorted. 'He would have no success with me.'

'You mean that there is hope for me yet?' he smiled.

'I did not say that, Reverend Christopher. I am waiting to discover if sisterly love for a gentleman would do in a wife,' she replied without hesitation.

'I think it would do very nicely. As soon as I have a parish, I will come to you again, Anna. I hope it will be soon. Father is making enquiries in the Keynsham area; there has been news of a vacancy at Compton Dando. It really depends on who is the patron of the living. Father is quite well known and highly respected.'

Anna looked at him curiously. 'Do you love me, Christopher? You have never said so.'

He gave a little frown. 'But you know I love you, Anna, have loved you for ever. Don't need to keep saying it.'

'Would you kiss me?'

'Kiss you? Before we are married? Not quite the thing, you know.'

Anna sighed. 'Just one little kiss,' she pleaded.

'Very well, against my principles, but I wish to please you.' And he bent towards her and his lips gently touched her cheek.

'Thank you, Christopher,' she managed to whisper feeling completely deflated. If her mother had kissed her, she would have felt no different. She wondered if all young gentlemen behaved as Christopher did . . . the unbidden vision of a proud Mr Peverill in the wood came into her mind only to be swiftly dismissed.

Anna's doubts about her affection for Christopher were soon forgotten in the promised trip to London and the purchase of yards of muslin, sarsenet and satin as well as a visit to a mantua-maker where a come-out dress for Anna and a gown for her mama were soon made up.

The come-out ball was fixed in the Upper Rooms at Bath for 21st June – they later learned that it was the very day of Lord Wellington's victory at the battle of Vitoria and the start of his march into France, taking San Sebastian, then swiftly across the border to Biarritz.

In all that time, there had been no news of Philippe Peverill. There had been constant exchanges between Ponderfields and Hatherley Park, but Anna found herself liking Thora Peverill no better.

On the occasion of them taking the invitation to the come-out ball to Hatherley Park, Mrs Starkie and Anna were welcomed and then treated to one of Miss Peverill's lengthy monologues.

'Do come in and I will order a little wine; it is quite late enough in the morning; or would you rather have a glass of ratafia, Mrs Starkie? I prefer wine myself, I buy only the best and it is sent from London. Our family has used the same wine merchant for many years, so we can always rely on the quality, you can be sure. Now what is this? Your come-out ball? Oh, my dear girl, how very splendid. And at the Upper Rooms, too. June 21st? Now I wonder if Philippe will be home by that time? There is never any knowing with my cousin. No word from him for weeks, then suddenly he is there again. I suppose I have become accustomed to it and I do not pry into his affairs. Am I allowed to ask about your gown, or are you keeping it a secret? Then you will surprise us with your beauty. Oh, how well I remember my own come-out at Almack's – Mama was well known to the patronesses, of course, and was a close friend of Lady Jersey. I wore white for I was only eighteen years of age and it was considered correct in a young girl. It seems like yesterday and I have waited ever since for my dear Philippe. I am sure he will declare himself now that he has a country property. He had no wish for us to live the whole year in the London house, splendid though it is. And I do so love it in the country, so close and gossipy, that is what I like. Formality doesn't do for me . . . let me pour you some more ratafia, Mrs Starkie . . . you must go? Oh, and you have not been here two minutes. But I feel honoured to be invited to your come-out, Anna, and I hope I have your permission to bring Philippe if he chances to be here. Thank you, thank you, such kindness. Let me ring for the maid to show you out. It has been a great pleasure. Goodbye.'

Outside the house and before they stepped up into the carriage, Anna looked at her mother. They both of them laughed heartily.

'What a woman,' said Anna. 'Can you imagine her all in white at Almack's? But I must not criticize for I am sure she is very good-hearted. Mama, we neither of us said a single word!'

'And to think that you scold me for talking too much,' replied Mrs Starkie. 'I will remind you of Thora Peverill another time.'

All was excitement on the day of the come-out ball; Felicity, Selina and Jane were allowed to be of the party as were the two younger Boyd boys, Jeremy and Matthew.

Everyone agreed that Anna looked lovely in a gown of cornflower blue – she had refused to wear white at the age of twenty years. The gown suited her fair curls and it was cut fashionably low in the bodice and trimmed with lace flowers of a paler blue around the sleeves and hem, and also twined in her hair.

Miss Thora Peverill, still without her cousin, was asked to sit with the rectory party and her never-ending flow of comments on the fashions and manners of the evening at least served to amuse the young people.

Anna found herself in constant demand for dances and she knew it was not because of her fortune, for they had managed to keep the size of her legacy a secret; in any case, most of her partners proved to be young gentlemen from the neighbourhood with whom she was well acquainted.

Christopher claimed her hand for the waltz – at least two waltzes were allowed during the evening – and she enjoyed being whirled around in his arms; they had practised the steps many times at Ponderfields. Christopher was no killjoy, but did whatever was proper; that night, he was proud to hold Anna around the waist for the waltz.

'That was very nice, Christopher,' Anna said to him, as they returned to their place. 'It was better than taking a turn around the drawing-room, was it not? I do believe that I shall have to sit out the next country dance I am so out of breath. But no, I cannot, here is Mr Shilton come to claim me. He is a quiet young man so

I shall not have much need to exert myself in trivial conversation.'

It was as she and Mr Shilton were going down the set for the last time, that Anna caught sight of a strange, tall figure standing in the doorway of the ballroom. The strangeness was not only because he seemed familiar to her, but that he was dressed in a greatcoat of elegant length and with several capes; he had dark hair and he carried a beaver hat in his hand.

Anna's footsteps almost faltered as she recognized Mr Philippe Peverill. He acknowledged her recognition by raising his fine head and making a small beckoning gesture.

'Are you quite well, Miss Starkie?' asked the quiet Mr Shilton. 'We will sit out the rest of the dance when we have reached the bottom of the set if you wish.'

'Yes, thank you,' Anna replied feebly. She felt out of breath and knew that it was not from the exertion of the country dance. But she made an excuse to her partner. 'I think I am still recovering from the last waltz.'

He led her to her place, made his bow and departed for his next partner.

But Anna did not sit down. She could think only of the commanding figure in the doorway; she looked again and saw him give a slight nod before turning away. He wishes to speak with me, she told herself, he could not come into the ballroom dressed in his outdoor clothes. Whatever shall I do? She looked around her; Christopher had gone off to claim his partner for the next dance and she saw that Miss Peverill was holding court to the rest of the party. They were nodding politely and the children were giggling.

Her feet carried her to the door; she hardly knew that she was moving, but she could still see ahead of her the dark and aristocratic head. She reached him, their eyes met and held. He put out his hand and almost without knowing what she was doing, Anna placed hers into his clasp.

'Miss Starkie, I had to come. There is a small card-room here that is unused at the moment, please give me a few moments of your company.'

'Mr Peverill,' was all she could find to say and she found herself quite alone with him in a small room, the only furniture being a few card tables with chairs around them.

'Mr Peverill,' she repeated, 'what are you doing here? And where have you been all this time? I should never have come in here on my own with you; I will say good evening and return to my family.'

'I will not compromise you, ma'am, I thought I would do you the honour of congratulating you on your come-out.'

It was said as haughtily as ever and she started to turn towards the door.

'No, Miss Starkie . . . Anna . . . just let me say a few words of explanation for my dress and for appearing at the Upper Rooms in all my dirt. I have been travelling all day and when I reached Hatherley Park, it was to find it empty of my cousin. Mrs Shapter – in her excitement and upset because I had appeared so unexpectedly – told me that it was Miss Anna's come-out ball at the Upper Rooms. Everyone was there, she told me. So I have come straight here from Hatherley Park. I found that I had looked forward to renewing our acquaintance. Then I had a desire to see you in a ball dress and not your plain country clothes. You look beautiful, Anna.'

But Anna was overwhelmed at the attention and her words came not as she would have wished them to if she had thought about it first.

'Balderdash, Mr Peverill, you have probably seen a dozen beautiful young ladies in sumptuous gowns in Weymouth these last weeks.'

His eyes narrowed, his head lifted. 'You think me insincere, ma'am?'

'If you had been sincere, sir, you would have complimented me on my looks and gone away.' Anna knew that she was being rude to him, but felt herself to be at a loss and not in command of her words.

'Anna, I thought you beautiful in your old blue pelisse, and I think you beautiful in your pretty ballgown. I mean it. Now, I will not embarrass you further and I will go . . . may I kiss you?'

'Sir?' Anna felt that she was frozen to the spot at his words, for suddenly a surge of feeling through her body was telling her that she wanted to be kissed by him.

She started to turn away. I must go before I commit an indiscretion, she told herself, I should not be in this room on my own with him, in any case. But she felt hands on her shoulders, pulling her gently towards him but not up against him.

She raised her eyes to his in protest and was shocked by a grey gleam of passion.

'You would not dare,' she almost hissed the words.

'I dare,' he murmured.

And he bent his lips to hers and let them linger for long moments. It was Anna's first kiss.

He lifted his head. 'Anna. . . .' he started to say, but was quickly interrupted.

'You are no gentleman, sir. I will return to your cousin, who is certainly no lady.'

And with stiff, proud words, she reached the door, walked into the vestibule and made her way unsteadily back to her family.

Miss Peverill immediately noticed her flushed and rebellious face and expression.

'Anna, wherever have you been? I trust that Mr Shilton did not take you apart from the ballroom, for it is not the done thing to be seen alone with a young gentleman, you know. I could wish that

Philippe had been here, for he would have kept guard over you. He is very proper, the last word in respectability. Oh, I know of the rumours that fly around West Wilton about him, but it is no more than the wagging of the tongues of a few country bumpkins. They do not know my cousin as I do. You would be more than safe in his company, I can assure you. Now come and sit by me and you can miss the next dance – it is the quadrille, I believe – and we can have a coze. . . .'

This tirade and Thora's outrageous words, and her opinion of her cousin's behaviour, succeeded in restoring Anna's sense of what was proper. She even managed to smile inwardly at what had happened in the little card-room and what histrionics Miss Peverill would have presented had she known.

THREE

IN SPITE OF the late hour of their return from Bath, Anna was at the breakfast-table at her usual time the next morning. She was alone, but she did not object to that as her come-out ball had given her much to think about. Not the least being the presumptious – indeed outrageous – behaviour of Mr Philippe Peverill. She blushed now for his temerity in taking her apart into one of the card-rooms, though she was able to appreciate that he had not wanted to be seen in his travelling clothes on such an occasion.

As for the audacious kiss, she decided that it was best forgotten. She believed it to have come from a man who was probably no more than a libertine and if, at the time, it had disturbed her feelings, then her only recourse was to put the incident out of her mind. And her heart, she added.

She rose from the breakfast-table and went into the empty drawing-room. The fire had been lit but she sat away from it as the June morning was very warm; her old cheese-paring instincts told her that there was no need for a fire, but then she smiled to herself for she knew her mother liked it and they could now afford its luxury.

Anna had only been there minutes, when a maid opened the door. 'Are you at home to Mr Peverill, Miss Anna?'

Astonishment made Anna rise up from her chair and stammer hastily, 'Yes . . . yes, please show him in, Peggy.'

And there stood Mr Philippe Peverill, resplendent in a blue superfine coat cut obviously by a master tailor, buff pantaloons and gleaming hessians; only his shirt points and neck-cloth proclaimed the dandy. The tilt of his head and the half-smile about his lips once again reminded her of Mr Darcy.

'Miss Starkie,' he murmured and bowed.

An imp of unbelievable mischief arose in Anna and her thoughts became words. 'Have you read *Pride and Prejudice*, Mr Peverill?'

'Ma'am?' It was almost an unspoken question.

'It is by the same lady who wrote *Sense and Sensibility* and it is all the rage. You remind me of Mr Darcy.'

'I have read the book, Miss Starkie, and I believe Mr Darcy to be very proud in his bearing.'

'Yes, that is my meaning,' Anna returned quickly.

'You like to jest, Miss Starkie? Or do you consider me proud?'

'You may not be at all proud in your character, sir, I do not know you well enough, but your stance is certainly a proud one.' Anna felt the incivility of her words and hardly knew what possessed her. I suppose I feel I must censure his behaviour of last evening, she told herself.

'Are you usually so forthright, Miss Starkie?' he enquired with a lift of his quizzing-glass.

'No, never. But then I have never met anyone quite like you before,' she replied coolly. 'It is not every day that a young lady gets taken into an empty room at the Upper Rooms and insulted with a kiss.'

'You felt insulted, ma'am? I must apologize, for I quite enjoyed the kiss and I thought for a moment that you did, too.'

Now he is fencing with me, Anna decided; how long can I keep this up? He is quite insufferable. 'My feelings have nothing to do with the matter, sir, the incident was nothing short of disgraceful and well you know it.'

Suddenly he smiled at her and Anna held her breath. His eyes were alight with mischief and a certain admiration which she thought was meant to flatter.

'Miss Starkie, I have come here this morning especially to apologize to you, and to tell you that my actions last night were completely unpremeditated. I had come to the Upper Rooms simply to give you my good wishes on your come-out, but when I saw you advancing down the set of the country dance, I was completely bewitched. My Cinderella had changed into the most beautiful girl I had ever seen. You chose to come to me and after that . . . I did not behave as a gentleman should. Will you accept my apology?'

Anna could not refuse. There was something about this man which fascinated her; it had led her into indiscretions in her choice of words, it had let her accept his kiss. She could have turned her face away but she had not.

I will try to be formal, she told herself. 'I appreciate your gesture in coming to Ponderfields this morning, Mr Peverill, and I accept your apology. I blame myself for leaving the safety of the ballroom in the first place. We were both at fault.'

He took a step towards her, reached for her hand and raised it to his lips. All through that exchange of words, they had remained standing, confronting each other as adversaries.

'You are gracious, Anna. I had thought it would be so and I am glad I am not mistaken. I may call you Anna?'

'My family call me Anna, I am usually known as Miss Starkie.'

'I stand rebuked, ma'am, I will remember in future. I hope there is to be a future, Miss Starkie,' he said smoothly.

'I do not think I understand your meaning, sir.'

'Let us sit down,' he said quietly. 'We cannot stand forever facing each other as though we were enemies.'

They still faced each other, but Anna sat in her chair and Mr Peverill on the ottoman.

'I have not come this morning solely to make my apologies,' he told her.

'Sir?' Anna queried, wondering what was coming next.

'I have my curricle waiting outside. It would please me very much if you would accompany me for a drive.'

Anna was astonished at his words and at the invitation which was spoken with great cordiality, without a hint of his previous stiffness.

She smiled. 'It would be very plesant,' she said, and found that she was quite sincere. She would enjoy a drive with this enigmatic gentleman who could change from formality to pleasantness in as many words. But she did wonder to herself about Christopher. He would be wanting to talk over the occasion of her ball, but it was usually much later in the morning or even the afternoon before he rode over from the rectory, so she tried not to feel guilty about him.

Mr Peverill had been quick to notice her little frown. 'Something bothers you, Miss Starkie,' he said to her, and his voice was amazingly kind.

'No, it is not exactly a bother, just the thought that Christopher Boyd might come over, but I can see him on my return.'

'Christopher from the rectory? You are perhaps betrothed to him?' he asked.

She shook her head. 'No, nothing like that though he would like it, I must confess.'

'Then I must not incur his jealousy.'

'I do not think a short drive in a curricle with a neighbour is likely to incur jealousy in someone like Christopher,' she answered him.

'Even though the neighbour has stolen a kiss?' he taunted her.

'That disgraceful episode is now forgotten and there is not likely to be a repeat of it, after all.'

'I would very much like to repeat it.'

'Your meaning, sir?' Anna's voice was starchy.

'I am finding it difficult not to kiss you again, my dear Anna.'

'I am certainly not your dear Anna, and if there is any talk like that, I will decline your offer of a drive.' If I continue to talk, Anna thought, I can keep him at a distance even though I have this unreasonable urge to be taken in his arms and held close. I must put it down to midsummer madness, it is 22 June after all. 'I will see Christopher this afternoon,' she told him. 'It is often his habit to come for dinner. Now I will fetch a light shawl, it is a warm day and I will not need a pelisse.'

She stood up and found herself close to him, her breath came quickly, but he did not attempt to touch her.

'I must assure you, Miss Starkie, that you are quite safe with me. The temptation is there – I too think it must be midsummer madness – but I have myself well in hand. Go and fetch your shawl and we will be off before the admirable Christopher arrives.'

Anna left the room in a daze; we even have the same thoughts, she was saying to herself, midsummer madness indeed. I suppose I am safer being driven in a curricle for his attention will be on tooling his horses.

At the gate, he helped her up into the curricle and jumped up beside her. 'Now where shall we go? The lanes are dry at this time of year so I do not think we will need to use the busy turnpike road. I have been talking to Mr Shapter this morning and he says that it is a pleasant drive to Wellow and that there is a Roman pavement there. Do you like to visit antiquities, Miss Starkie? I have yet to see the Roman baths in the city.'

He is surprising me again, Anna was thinking; who would have thought him to be interested in history?

'We were taken to Wellow when we were children, but I hardly remember it though the countryside is pleasant. If you are interested in ancient things, Mr Peverill, we must organize an expedition to Stanton Drew. There is a splendid stone circle there, though I believe it not to be as spectacular as the one at Avebury which you may have seen.'

He glanced down at her. 'I do believe that you are accepting me and including me as a resident already, Miss Starkie; it is most encouraging. I would indeed like to see the stone circle; we must try and get there before the summer is over. My cousin Thora is not very interested in such things though she would not like to be excluded from an expedition.' He paused. 'I am afraid I never know when I am going to be called away, but Thora is used to it and manages very well. She did not really wish to be moved into the country, but she seems to have settled very well and made herself quite part of the local scene. You like my cousin, Miss Starkie?'

I will have to pretend, said Anna to herself. 'She is excessively sociable and is invited everywhere. She very soon asked us to dine at Hatherley Park and we were disappointed to find that you had been called away. But she made us feel very welcome.'

'She has a good heart and her only fault is that she never stops talking. She must sometimes think that I have turned deaf for I never listen to a word she says. However, I must not criticize her for she is an excellent housekeeper.'

And wife? thought Anna. I still find it hard to imagine, though Miss Peverill does seem certain that one day she will be Mrs Philippe Peverill.

'She always refers to you as *Philippe* in the French way. You have a French name, Mr Peverill?'

'Yes, indeed,' he answered her directly. 'Not surprising, because my mother is French. She comes of a very old French family, the Poincarés; they lived in Paris and my father met her during his Grand Tour. This was all before the Revolution of course. *Maman* was quite happy to live in London and she became a society beauty; after my father died, she returned to live in Paris and I see very little of her since we have been at war. But she did insist that I grew up speaking both languages, and I have always been glad of that—' he stopped almost as though he had said too much. Then he looked at her and continued. 'Do you speak French, Miss Starkie?'

Anna nodded. 'Yes, just a little and not very fluently, I am afraid. I had a mamselle as a governess for a short while and I learned from her. She insisted that we talked only in French when we went on our walks.'

'You have brothers and sisters?'

'I did have two little brothers but they died when they were quite young. There was a gap after that and then came Felicity, Selina and Jane who are still in the schoolroom. They were allowed to come to the Upper Rooms last night, but of course, you would not have seen them.'

He slowed the curricle and was looking around him. 'I think I can see Wellow church in the distance. Mr Shapter said that the site of the Roman villa is marked in a field just before you get as far as the church, so let us look out.'

The field was easily found and Mr Peverill helped her down from the curricle. 'Are you wearing sensible shoes?' he asked her, and held on to her hand.

'I would hardly be wearing dancing pumps to come into the country,' she said tartly. 'These are my half-boots; I wear them for our walks.'

'*We* meaning you and Christopher?'

'No, you are quite wrong,' and she almost added, for once, but thought it impertinent. 'I sometimes take a morning walk with Miss Swinburne – she is the governess – and my sisters.'

They reached the field and found the site of the Roman villa marked by four upright stones, but there was little sign of the tessellated pavement they had hoped to see.

'I think you will see more in Bath, Mr Peverill,' said Anna as they regained the curricle.

'Yes, maybe, but I have had the pleasure of a drive in pretty Somerset countryside and with excellent company, I might add.'

'Doing it too brown, sir, you would have done better with your cousin,' she replied.

'I would have drowned in words,' he laughed, and Anna joined in, wondering if, after all, there lurked a sense of humour in that complex nature; Philippe Peverill had certainly shown a different side to his character that day, and Anna found that it was an aspect of their new neighbour she could come to like.

The late summer months were spent very pleasantly, with assemblies and routs in Bath interspersed with riding parties, trips in the curricle and at last, the planned expedition to Stanton Drew. During all this time, Anna had enjoyed the company of Philippe Peverill though she was rarely on her own with him. Thora accompanied him everywhere. He would be missing for days at a time and Anna became accustomed to his sudden reappearance, learning not to ask about his absence or his whereabouts. The gossips had it that he was sometimes seen on the London road, but more often on the way to Weymouth.

By the end of August, with the fall of San Sebastian, the news from the Peninsula was good with the expectation that Lord Wellington would soon be pushing Marshal Soult and the French Army eastward into France.

Anna was determined on the Stanton Drew expedition before

the darker evenings came upon them. But Philippe had been missing for over a week and Christopher was busy settling himself into the parish he had secured at Battiscombe near the Wiltshire border. He would be vicar of the parish which included a handsome Elizabethan vicarage and he had done his best to persuade Anna to marry him before he took up residence.

They had not quarrelled over it, but Christopher had gone off to Battiscombe leaving Anna feeling unsettled.

On the evening before his departure, they walked along the stream behind the rectory for the last time.

'I wish you were coming with me as my wife,' Christopher said and he sounded wistful. 'Can I make you change your mind at the last minute, Anna?'

She shook her head. 'It would not be honest of me to pretend to love you, Christopher.'

'I hope it is not your fortune which has come between us,' he said.

'Christopher, you know my views on the money I inherited, and you are the only one who does know apart from Mama. The money has made us comfortable and free from financial worries and debt and no more. I know you well enough, to understand that the money would make no difference if we loved one another. In any case, you asked me to be your wife when I was penniless! I have the feeling that you will suddenly fall in love and feel glad that I have not accepted you. Perhaps you will meet someone in Battiscombe; there is probably a young lady there just waiting to be loved by the new vicar.'

Christopher had to laugh. 'Oh, Anna, you do not change, but I will not give up hope. Battiscombe is only five or six miles away and I will often visit Father and Mother and promise to come and see you. But, Anna, tell me truthfully: what about Philippe Peverill?'

'Philippe Peverill?' she echoed. 'What about him?'

'We have often been in his company these last weeks and I have seen him looking at you sometimes.'

'Whatever do you mean? You know as well as I do that he is firmly attached to his cousin. She is like a limpet! Do you know that I have never once been on my own with him since he took me in his curricle to Wellow. And that was weeks and weeks ago now.'

'And do you want to be on your own with him, Anna?'

'It is not my habit to break up a betrothal between a gentleman and the lady he has asked to be his wife,' Anna said forcefully.

'I notice that you do not say *the lady he loves*.'

'No, I do not. I will be honest and say that I don't think he does love her, it is all on her side. But he seems satisfied with the arrangement and she is very tolerant about his strange absences.'

'I wonder if she knows what goes on?' he grinned.

'Christopher, that is not like you. For you are suggesting that his business trips are somewhat improper.'

'No, I am sorry, I have been listening to local gossip and that does not become the new vicar of Battiscombe, does it?'

'It does not. I am ashamed of you.' Anna smiled up at him. 'But you will make a splendid vicar, you are so *nice*. And the whole of Battiscombe will be queuing up at the vicarage door for your help and sympathy.'

'You are guilty of levity, Anna. I intend to be a very proper vicar.' He looked down at her. 'May I kiss you goodbye?' he asked.

'Do you really want to, it is not very proper.'

'Yes, I do,' he replied, and pulled her into his arms and kissed her on the cheek just as he had done before. Remembering another kiss, Anna was glad of the sweet pleasantness of Christopher's. And she gave him a sisterly hug and wished him every success and happiness in Battiscombe.

Anna thought it strange that on the very day after this farewell conversation, and with Christopher on his way, that Philippe Peverill should call upon her. He was in an odd mood.

She was sitting in the drawing-room already missing Christopher and feeling sad – then laughing at herself for her fickle sentiments – when Mr Peverill was announced.

It had been their custom, to meet up at Hatherley Park and for Anna and Christopher to make up a foursome with Mr Peverill and his cousin.

That day, he gave a stiff bow to Mrs Starkie who was busy at some netting and looked pointedly at Anna.

'Come into the garden, Anna, I wish to speak to you.'

It was spoken as a command and although Anna bristled at his tone, she did not argue and followed him out of the room. They stood together under the trees which sheltered the house from the lane which ran into the village.

'Christopher has gone?' were his first words.

She nodded. 'Yes, I said goodbye to him yesterday and he set off for Battiscombe at first light this morning. He will be there by now.'

'I thought you might be sad at his going so I have come to ask you to ride with me.'

Anna felt astonished and must have shown her astonishment.

'You look amazed, Anna, are you not able to credit me with a kind gesture?' he asked, and his tone was more formal.

'I am sorry, Mr Peverill,' she replied hastily. 'It is so exceedingly kind of you and very thoughtful. When you were announced, I was thinking of Christopher and of how much I would miss him. But where is your cousin?'

'Thora is at Hatherley Park. We have not quarrelled, but the fact is that I do not always wish for her company. Do you realize that in these last weeks, I have never once been on my own with you?'

She gazed at him and then could only stammer, 'B-but that is just what I said to Christopher last night.'

She saw him stiffen and called herself a fool for saying such a thing to him.

'So you discussed me with the Reverend Christopher? I hope he had good advice to offer you.' His words were not short of a heavy sarcasm.

'I am sorry, Mr Peverill, I think Christopher was hoping that I would continue in the company of you and your cousin once he had gone.'

'And your reply?'

'I said that it was not my habit to intrude upon the betrothal of a gentleman and a lady. . . .'

'There is no betrothal.'

Anna took a deep breath. 'What are you saying, Mr Peverill? Miss Thora has told us many times that she is to be your wife.'

'Thora is presuming too much.' He was angry now. 'It is true that our families planned a marriage between us, but it is also true that I do not feel committed.'

Anna regretted her next words as soon as she had spoken them. 'But Miss Peverill implied that she was a lady of some substance and that you needed her fortune . . . oh, I am sorry, I should not have said that. Do forgive me.'

'Miss Starkie, you seem to be unfortunate in your choice of words and I very much regret that you have seen fit to indulge in gossip over me. What else am I accused of?' His tone was like steel and Anna knew that she would have to be at her most prudent not to provoke an argument.

'Mr Peverill, I had no wish to offend. There is a lot of speculation about your absences from Hatherley Park and I am always quick to defend you, but your cousin has an unfortunate habit of speaking at length upon everything; nothing is sacred to her. I confess, sometimes it is not easy to bear with her conversation. I am being very forthright, but that is my nature and if you have no wish for my company, I will bid you good-day.'

Anna turned as though to walk back to the house, but found her arm grasped closely and she was forced to stop.

'Miss Starkie, I must ask you something and I want you to be honest with me. I know my cousin's tongue, but have always thought it harmless, indeed I think I once told you that I hardly listen to what she has to say. But tell me this, Anna, and I rely on you for the truth. As you say yourself, you are very forthright. What is said in the village about my absences from Hatherley Park? I wish to know particularly.'

There was an underlying seriousness, even an urgency, in his question. For some reason, it is important to him, she thought. 'I will make a simple list and then you will see why I never heed the gossips. It is said that you have a mistress in Weymouth; that you are a French spy; that you go to London on business; that you were profligate in your youth and have to marry a lady of some fortune; and I have also heard that you have been seen along the Dorset coast and are probably a smuggler.'

His roar of laughter startled her and she felt like joining in when she saw the unexpected amusement in his eyes.

'And which one would you prefer to believe, Anna?'

She did not hesitate. 'That you have squandered a fortune and are obliged to marry an heiress.'

'What an unexpected reply,' he said, still amused. 'Have you a reason for choosing that piece of gossip?'

She nodded. 'As a matter of fact, I have, Mr Peverill, but I have no intention of elaborating on it.'

'You are a strange girl. I want to ask you something else.'

'Sir?'

'Could you not try to call me Philippe?'

She was surprised at the question and answered quickly. 'No, I do not think so, Mr Peverill.'

'And have you a reason?' he asked her.

'I have two reasons. First of all, I do not think our acquaintance sufficiently advanced to be addressing each other by our first names, and secondly, I think that your cousin would be upset at the familiarity; I do not wish to offend her.'

He was silent and stared down at her, almost as though he was trying to weigh up her reply. Then he remarked quite pleasantly and very lightly, 'Very well, Miss Starkie, it seems excessively formal, but I will only call you Anna when the occcasion merits it. Now all this talking and you have not answered the question I first asked you. I have come for that particular purpose. Will you ride with me? I am assuming that you have a mount. I have heard gossip, too, and I know of your recent legacy and that there are ponies for your sisters in your stables, and a fine mare for you.'

'You cousin keeps you well informed, Mr Peverill.'

'It has proved to my advantage this time. Have you indeed acquired a mare?'

Anna could keep up the formal barrier between them no longer. It had been extremely kind of him to consider her sadness at losing Christopher, and she would love a good gallop above all things.

'I have Corinna, yes,' she told him.

'That is an unusual name for a horse,' he remarked.

Anna nodded. 'Yes, I like unusual names, perhaps because I have such a plain one myself. I looked up a book of classical myths and Corinna is the Greek for maiden so I thought it appropriate for a young mare.'

'And do you think that Corinna would like a ride today?'

She smiled. 'Yes, I do indeed. It is most kind of you to think of it. Have you left your horse in the stables? Is he a hunter?'

'Yes, he is a fine hunter, but I am afraid he does not possess a fine name. I call him Jack!'

They both laughed and Anna felt easier. 'I must go and put on my riding-dress; perhaps you could go and ask Jem, the stable-boy, to saddle Corinna for me.'

'Certainly, ma'am,' he smiled, and walked away in the direction of the stables.

They met up at the gate and decided to ride in the direction of Combe Down which was an open moor high above Bath, with very fine views of the city and an ideal place for horse-riding.

Nothing was said between them as they reached the open countryside and Anna felt strangely content. She had not been as far as this since acquiring Corinna and was more than happy to ride alongside the silent Mr Peverill.

As Combe Down came into view, he looked down at her. 'Race you to the top,' he said with mischief in his voice.

'It is no contest,' she protested. 'A hunter like Jack will outstrip Corinna easily.'

'I will give you a minute's start,' he told her.

She grinned up at him. 'Done,' she said, dug in her heels and Corinna was flying to the top of the down.

Anna did not know when she had enjoyed a gallop more and was not in the least surprised when she was overtaken by Jack and his rider a hundred yards before they reached the top. There, at a clump of trees, Philippe Peverill had dismounted and was waiting for her. He held out his arms and Anna slid off Corinna's back straight into his waiting embrace.

Panting with the exertion, she looked up at him with a laugh . . . what she saw in his eyes gave her a shock. A warmth, an admiration were there and then he was murmuring her name. 'Anna,' he breathed, 'do not call me Mr Peverill, say my name.'

'Philippe,' she whispered, and it seemed only natural for him to pull her close and let his lips take the second kiss of their acquaintance.

Anna felt the magic of it again just as she had done in the little card-room on the night of her come-out. She must defend herself with words, or put her arms around his neck to draw him closer. This latter was forbidden to her.

She raised her head. 'You take kisses very easily, sir,' she said with some acerbity.

'You tempt me into kissing you, my dear Anna, and you did call me Philippe a moment ago. I thought it was an invitation.'

'I regret it and it was certainly no invitation. It seemed to give you the permission to behave as no gentleman should. That is the second time that I have had cause to say that very thing. I think perhaps we had better ride home.'

Anna had the odd feeling that she was close to tears and she turned away from him to try and hide it. He must have seen her emotion for he spoke with a sudden cheerful common sense.

'The kiss was no more than a thank you for a really splendid gallop and for bringing me to this lovely place. What a beautiful city Bath is, perched on its high hills. I am very fortunate indeed to be the present owner of Hatherley Park.'

Anna followed the commonsense behind his words and was grateful. 'I thought you must have chosen Hatherley especially to be close to Bath,' she said, and was puzzled at a fleeting frown that crossed his eyes and also why he had described himself as the *present* owner almost as though he did not intend to make it his permanent home.

'One cannot always choose where one will be in life and I think this time I have been fortunate.'

What an enigmatic remark, Anna was thinking; but then he was helping her on to Corinna and they rode home quickly in amicable silence.

The silence was rudely broken as they reached the stables at Ponderfields, for who should come running from the house but Miss Thora Peverill.

'Philippe.' His name was shrieked out in anger. 'How dare you go off riding without my knowledge. I guessed that you were here and rode over to find you. There is an urgent message for you. You know very well what our arrangements have to be.'

FOUR

An astonished Anna gazed from Mr Philippe Peverill to his cousin. She could see a stiff anger in his expression.

'Thora, you know very well that you should not have come here talking about messages. Can I ever hope to curb your tongue? Stay and talk to Anna while I ride back to Hatherley, and please guard your words.' He turned to Anna and she saw that the former reserve had reappeared in his expression. 'Good-day, Miss Starkie, and my thanks for the pleasure of the ride to Combe Down.'

Their eyes met and behind the stern look, Anna seemed to read the words *and the kiss*.

He was gone and Anna was confronted by a very voluble Thora Peverill.

'Anna, where have you been? And where is Combe Down? There was I looking everywhere for Philippe only to go to the stables and be told that he had gone out on Jack. And with not a word to me. I was never more upset. So I had to think hard about where he might be and I am sorry to say that I could only come to the conclusion that he had come to Ponderfields. It has not passed my notice that he has been particular in his attentions to you when we have all been out together. So it was not hard for me to work out that with Christopher gone off to Battiscombe yesterday, you would be on your own this morning.' These last words were said with a sense of triumph, Anna thought.

'So having fathomed that, I had only to decide whether to come on foot through the park or to bring the gig. I thought the walk would be too fatiguing, so here I am. And when your mama told me that you had gone off riding with Philippe, I was outraged. I had thought you to be sly, but to go riding with a gentleman already spoken for, I could hardly believe. What do you mean by it all? You lose Christopher and turn immediately to Philippe. It is hardly the behaviour of a lady. I would expect better of a Starkie ... well, what have you to say for yourself, you have not spoken a word since Philippe left us.

Anna nearly choked with laughter at this last statement, for Thora had not paused once. But she knew that here was a very jealous woman and that she would have to choose her words carefully.

'Miss Peverill, I am sorry that you have been upset—' but Anna was not even allowed to finish her sentence.

'Upset? That does not by any means describe my feelings. I am angry and outraged, as I said before. Philippe is very precious to me and I will brook no interference in my affairs. Are you going to offer me an apology for your appalling behaviour?'

Take a deep breath, Anna, the woman is barely rational, she thought. 'Miss Peverill, if I have unwittingly offended you, indeed I am very sorry. I do not know Mr Peverill well, but I thought it exceedingly kind of him to invite me to ride out with him this morning because he thought of my sadness at losing Christopher. Christopher has been as a dearest brother to me. I cannot remember a moment of my life when he was not at my side. It was always expected by our two families that we should marry, but you will understand my feelings on the matter when I say that one does not marry a favourite brother.' She paused and thought she was doing well with not another word from Miss Peverill. 'So there was I this morning, feeling very low-spirited, and your cousin was most thoughtful. We did not ride far, but I have a new mare, Corinna.'

'That is a ridiculous name for a horse.'

'Yes, ma'am, I suppose it is, but it suits her.' I am certainly not going to make the explanation to Miss Peverill which her cousin understood so easily. 'We simply had a gallop to the top of Combe Down and back again, Combe Down is one of the high spots overlooking Bath. I did not think that we were gone very long and I am sorry to occasion such anxiety in you. Mr Peverill's business must have been urgent that you had to go looking for him.' Anna wondered what the response to this would be for Miss Peverill had received a stern caution from Philippe.... She stopped herself hastily; there, I am thinking of him as Philippe. I must be more careful or sparks will fly again.

But her last statement had registered with Miss Peverille. As he had ridden off, her cousin had told her to guard her words. How is she going to reply to this, Anna asked herself.

It was a somewhat chastened Miss Peverill who spoke again. 'It was nothing important, some matter with his lawyer, but it worried me that I had no idea where he was. Perhaps you have no notion what it is to be deeply attached to someone, Miss Starkie, you are very young.'

'Yes, I think I do understand for I am attached to Christopher even if we are not betrothed. Now, having mentioned Christopher again, I must tell you that he is coming back early next week and we are planning to make the expedition to Stanton Drew; we have been promising ourselves to do it for a long time. Mr Peverill is keen to see the stone circle and I hope it will please you . . . do you think I might call you Thora? And do call me Anna. Mr Peverill is always very formal, but I am sure we need not be.' It is a lie, thought Anna, but I must try and keep the peace.

She seemed to have succeeded for Thora Peverill managed a smile. 'I would indeed like to be included in the expedition,' she said quite pleasantly. 'I will go now and tell Philippe of the plans, unless he has had to rush off to London, of course.'

Anna watched her drive off in the gig. Something does not ring true, she told herself, she is devoted to him but the devotion is obviously not returned. I wonder if Philippe has any intention of marrying her for he seems to have not the least affection for her. And Anna resolutely put from her mind, the scene under the trees at Combe Down.

In the end, and after Philippe's return from London – or Weymouth, Anna was not sure which – it was a party of six who made up the expedition to Stanton Drew. They travelled in two vehicles: Christopher took his gig and had his brothers Jeremy and Matthew with him; and Mr Peverill's curricle was driven expertly by Miss Peverill with Anna as her passenger. Philippe rode Jack alongside them. Anna thought wickedly that Thora had had the arrangement of all this in order to ensure that Anna was at her side and not with Philippe.

The nearest village to the ancient stone circle was Pensford, but the lanes approaching Pensford were poor and the drivers took their time.

The rectory boys had been there before and were proud to show off their knowledge to the newcomers to the area.

The stones were impressive; originally a circle of standing stones, some were still upright and some were fallen – all were massive.

'You've got to see the Hauteville Quoit, it's colossal,' said Matthew – at the age of ten, knowledgeable and excitable. 'It is supposed to have been thrown by Sir John Hauteville from that hill up there that's called Maes Knoll – I don't know why. It's over a mile away and they say that the Quoit weighs about thirty tons.'

'When were the stones placed in the circle, Matthew?' asked Philippe, again showing a kindness which had surprised Anna before on the day after Christopher's departure.

'They are supposed to be Druid remains, sir, but I think they are Bronze Age. Somewhere I read that they were put there before the Egyptians built the Great Pyramid and that was thousands of years ago. They are like Avebury circle and Stonehenge, Mr Peverill; have you been there?'

Philippe nodded as he walked around the stones, Thora not far from his side; Anna was chatting happily to Christopher.

'Yes,' Philippe told Matthew. 'I have seen Avebury and Stonehenge, they are very well known. But I must say that your Somersetshire stone circle is very impressive. Does it have a legend attached to it? There is usually some story of how stones of this size could have been brought here.'

Matthew did know and told them all with some glee. 'It is a local tale,' he said. 'It is said that a village wedding took place on a Sunday and it was considered so wicked to be dancing on a Sunday, that the dancers were all turned to stone. It is quite ridiculous, of course, for we know that the stones were here long before we had any Sunday observance.'

Even Thora joined in the laughter and the two younger boys persuaded her to go and see Hauteville's Quoit with them; she obligingly followed.

Christopher was wandering around the outer circle of the stones and Anna suddenly found herself alone with Philippe. At least there is no danger of kisses today, she thought, and she smiled up at him.

'It is very interesting indeed, Anna; thank you for bringing us. Even Thora seems interested and she is really quite a philistine.'

'That is not very complimentary, Philippe,' she replied.

'Hoorah!'

'Whatever are you saying hoorah for?' she asked him. What an unpredictable man he was. Sometimes so proud and haughty, sometimes angry, and now joking with her.

'You called me "Philippe". Is this a special occasion?'

'No, it is not,' she said crossly. 'But we are on an expedition and we are enjoying ourselves, so I suppose it is not a time to be formal.'

'If there was no one else amongst these huge stones, would you let me be very informal with you?'

Anna looked at him; it was impossible to understand him. 'You are trying to shock me with a threat of disgraceful behaviour ... no, you cannot hold my hands, or kiss me, here is Thora.'

Thora came up with the boys and looked at Philippe suspiciously. 'Have I caught you flirting with Anna? It will not do, Philippe.'

Anna saw what she called his "Mr Darcy" look come over his face. 'Thora, how can you possibly imagine that I would behave in such a way. You know that you have my utmost devotion. And Anna is no more than a little slip of a thing; she seems not a lot older than Jeremy here.' He turned to the expectant boy. 'Jeremy, would you and Matthew take me to see this famous Quoit which was thrown from such a great distance?' And he walked off leaving an amused Anna and an unamused Thora whose voice had a prickly edge to it.

'Sometimes I cannot understand my cousin. I have known him all these years and yet there are times when he speaks to me as though I was a complete stranger. I am sorry that I accused you of flirting, Anna, I can see now that Philippe sees you as no more than a child. You are probably not a lot older than—'

Thora stopped short and Anna saw a peculiar look of horror and confusion in her face; it was not the first time that Thora had stopped speaking in mid-sentence and it only served to tell Anna that there seeeemed to be something that both Philippe and his cousin were trying to cover up. I do not suppose that I shall ever know the truth, thought Anna, but in future I will listen carefully to what they have to say.

But Anna was to have no chance of doing this, for in less than two weeks, Philippe was missing again. And in the time that followed, with Christmas and the New Year of 1814 upon them, nothing was heard of him.

The letters from John Boyd were optimistic, although written in atrocious cold and wet winter conditions, poised on the Pyrenees. It was Lord Wellington's objective, he told them, to push Soult and his army eastward into France, aiming for Toulouse and then Paris. Napoleon had suffered a humiliating defeat at Leipzig just as winter was creeping up on them.

Anna missed Christopher very much, and with Philippe also away, she found herself with Thora Peverill as an almost constant companion. When Philippe was not there, Thora could forget about jealousy and she seemed to put herself out to make a friend of Anna.

It began with them taking a walk each day and this would usually be across the extensive parkland of Hatherley. And on days when the ground was not hard with ice, or muddy from the rains, they would ride up to Combe Down.

Thora talked as much as ever, and Anne found herself in sympathy with Philippe for she, too, only half-listened to what was said. Sometimes a single word would make her prick up her ears, and gradually she thought she was piecing together a picture of the proud Mr Peverill.

'Do you have letters from Mr Peverill, Thora?' Anna asked the older woman on one of their walks. It was a blustery day in late December and they had sought the shelter of the wood. Anna never entered it without remembering her first sight of Philippe Peverill.

'Never.' The reply was cold and short.

Anna was nonplussed. The single word was unexpected and she did not know quite what to say next. 'You do not know his whereabouts then?' I am prying, Anna thought.

'I believe him to be in Weymouth.'

This brevity of speech was so unlike Thora that Anna wondered if Philippe did have a mistress in Weymouth. If it was so, then Thora would certainly not be pleased. Shall I delve a little deeper, Anna asked herself, even though Thora is in an unusually taciturn mood?

'And when do you plan your marriage? You did speak to me of it once, but I have never mentioned it since. However, we have become such good friends, that I feel I can ask you anything now.'

'We have no plans made. Philippe is a widower; I do not think it is his wish to rush into another marriage too quickly.'

Anna felt the rush of shock. It had never occurred to her that Philippe had once been married. He seemed very much the bachelor apart from his attachment to Thora. And had not Thora said that the family had always hoped for an alliance between herself and her cousin?

Anna could not stop her next words. 'But, Thora, I thought a marriage had been planned by the family for you and Philippe.'

Unusually Thora looked at a loss, then she launched into one of her long speeches. 'I have told you before that Philippe was rather wild in his youth, though you would not think it to see him now. He married when he was too young and his wife died in childbirth. He became even wilder after that and has only settled himself again these last few years. I pride myself on having a good influence on him, Anna. I know I was angry when he went riding with you that day, but when I thought it over, I said to myself "Thora, you must be pleased that Philippe had the kindness to think of Anna being sad at Christopher's going". That is my good influence, I said to myself. And now you and I have become friends and I have been grateful for your company. I do busy myself with the running of Hatherley Park, but it is very nice to have a companion in whom I can confide.'

'And do you expect Philippe home for Christmas, Thora? It is only a few days away now.'

There was a silence and Anna wondered if she was going to receive a reply. Thora will feel upset if Philippe chooses to stay in Weymouth, she thought.

The reply came at last and was both short and terse. 'I really do not know, Anna.'

'You are very welcome to spend Christmas Day at Ponderfields, Thora, I know that Mama would say the same. And maybe you would like to attend service with us; there is no need for you to be on your own if Philippe has not returned.'

'You are more than kind, Anna, and I will gladly accept your invitation. I would like to come if Philippe has not returned during the next few days.'

In the end, it was well into 1814 before Philippe came home. When he did come, he was very ill.

Thora arrived at Ponderfields soon after breafast one cold morning in late January; Anna found her looking worried and far from being her usual ebullient self.

'Thora, whatever is it? You look worried.'

'Anna, please will you come? I have brought the gig to be quick ... it is Philippe....'

'He is home?' Anna almost fired her question at Thora.

'Yes, he came last night after dark and he is quite ill and he keeps calling your name. I try and tell him it is Thora, but he takes no notice and just says "Anna, I must see Anna". Do you know why he should ask for you? Please, will you come?'

Anna nodded. 'Yes, of course I will come, but I cannot understand why he should ask for me. You must send for Mr Nesom from Bath, Thora, he is an excellent physician and Mama always has him to my sisters if they are ill. Let me fetch my pelisse and bonnet and I think I will need my muff today. I must also tell Mama where I am. I will join you in the gig in a few minutes. I am sorry you had to come with such bad tidings.'

At Hatherley, Anna wrote down the direction of the physician and Thora sent one of the stable boys off with a message. Then she followed Thora upstairs to Philippe's bedroom where she found him lying on top of the bed, fully clothed and covered with just a quilt.

Anna stood in shock at the sight of him. His face was almost grey in colour and his handsome features had become the drawn lines of illness.

She looked at Thora. 'He should be undressed and his face bathed.' She put a tentative hand to his forehead. 'He is burning, Thora; it must be a terrible fever.'

'What shall I do, Anna?'

Anna looked at the usually capable Thora and thought she should take charge; she had told Thora she was used to nursing her sisters.

'We must get him undressed and made more comfortable,' she said briskly.

Thora looked at her in horror. 'But we cannot undress him, Anna, he is a man.'

If Anna had not felt so worried, she would have laughed aloud. But it was no time for laughing. 'Does Philippe not have a manservant?' she asked.

'Yes, but Pierre was not with him and I don't know why. Philippe came on his own.'

'He was in the carriage?'

'No, on horseback.'

'He was not fit to be riding in this state. Thora, go and fetch Mr Shapter quickly. I know he is elderly but he can turn his hand to anything and he will know what to do. And while you are downstairs, tell Mrs Shapter to make a saline draught – oh, don't look like that, Thora, she will know what to do. We have got to get some fluids into him somehow – quickly now and then you had better leave it to me.'

'Yes, Anna,' said Thora, as she hurried off. She had never said so few words.

While Thora was out of the room, Anna bent over the still figure of Philippe, his breathing was shallow and she thought that a bad sign.

'Philippe.' Anna did not whisper, she spoke calmly and clearly. 'Philippe, it is Anna.'

She waited, but there was no response.

She touched his hands and forehead again; they were burning with a fever. Then she decided that she could at least take the quilt from him and undo his neckcloth and waistcoat. By the time she had done this, Thora had appeared with Mr Shapter. She gave a sigh of relief when she saw that Mrs Shapter followed with a jug containing the saline draught she had made.

'Thank you, Mrs Shapter. Miss Peverill and I will wait outside while Mr Shapter makes Mr Peverill more comfortable. Do you think you can find a nightshirt?'

Anna took Thora's arm and led her on to the landing.

'I'm sorry, Anna, I am not of much use in a sick-room,' Thora said, in a disturbed voice.

'Do not worry, you can leave it to me and Mrs Shapter. You can sit with Philippe when he is getting better. And, Thora, do you not think it would be better if I stayed here with you for a night or two?'

Thora look relieved, but Anna thought there was something strange in her expression. She must be worried about Philippe, Anna was saying to herself; she seems to have no experience at all of tending to someone who is ill.

'I will send a message to your mama,' Thora said. 'Perhaps you could make a list of the things you will need, and one of the servants will bring back a bag for you. I will send Poll, she is a sensible girl and can go in the dog-cart. Jude can take her, he is the eldest of the stable boys and has taken a fancy to Poll so he will not mind. I do not know how to thank you, Anna, you are so very capable.'

She was interrupted by Mr Shapter. 'He be more comfortable now, and the wife says as how she thinks one of you had better try to give him a drink. He has started thrashing about an' all. Looks quite queer he does, poor gentleman.'

Anna turned to Thora and when she saw her worried expression, she did not hesitate. 'Thora, you go down with Mr and Mrs Shapter and have some hot tea or coffee. This has all been a shock to you. I will sit with Mr Peverill and get him to drink some of the draught. But first, Mr Shapter, will you get some extra pillows and prop him up? That will make it easier for me.'

They all seemed glad for her to be in charge of things and no protests came from Thora. Mr Shapter did as she had asked, and Mrs Shapter took Thora downstairs.

Philippe was restless in his fever. His arms were thrashing about just as Mr Shapter had said; he kept muttering but it was all unintelligible.

She sat at his side and took up the mug which Mrs Shapter had left. 'Philippe, it is Anna. I want you to have a drink.'

For a second he was still and she thought he had recognized her voice, then a stream of words came from his lips. She thought it was gibberish until she realized that he was talking in French and too quickly for her to understand, although she could pick out the names of *Maman* and *Pierre*.

She put her hand on his shoulder and raised the mug to his lips forcing some of the liquid into him.

This went on for over an hour, but there was little change; he did not know her and the nonsense came continually from his lips, sometimes in French, sometimes in English when she thought she could pick out the same words over and over again.

At about twelve o'clock, Mr Nesom came. Thora brought him in looking anxious.

'Is he talking, Anna?' she asked.

Anna nodded. 'He never stops, but it is gibberish, and sometimes in French which is not surprising. The only words I can understand are *Maman* and *Pierre*.'

Mr Nesom asked for Mr Shapter and the ladies left the room. When they returned, they found the physician shaking his head. 'It is hard to understand, Miss Peverill. It has all the symptoms of typhus, but as far as I know there is no typhus in this country except sometimes in redcoats who have been sent home sick from the Peninsula. I think we must assume that it is a very bad dose of influenza. I have had many cases in Bath this winter. All I can tell you is to continue with the saline draught – it was very astute of you to think of that, Miss Anna. The fever will break very soon, but you must continue with the drinks. I have cupped him so that should improve his condition. I will come again tomorrow morning, but please send for me if you are worried.'

Thora saw the physician out and Anna sat down at Philippe's side again; he was quiet and she thought it must be due to the cupping.

There was little change that day, and in the night, Mrs Shapter and Anna took it turns to sit with him. Thora was solicitous but not anxious to go near the sick-room. Anna had never known her so quiet. She is worrying that Philippe will not make a recovery, Anna thought, she is very attached to him but cannot feel herself up to nursing him.

Just as it was getting light next morning, Anna thought that there had come a change in Philippe. His forehead, which she bathed continually, seemed a little cooler and he was not so restless.

Then suddenly his ramblings were less wild and she could pick out words including her own name. Her heart gave a leap when he took a drink without her having to force it and getting a lot of the liquid over his nightshirt.

Every so often, she would say his name and then very clearly 'Philippe, it is Anna, do you know me?'

There came the magic moment when he went still and said her name. 'Anna, I am sorry, Anna.'

'Philippe, I am here, say my name again.'

But it was too much to hope for; he fell silent and seemed to be asleep. Anna ran downstairs to find Thora who was in the breakfast-room sipping coffee. She turned as Anna hurried in.

'Not bad news, Anna, please say it is not bad news.'

Anna bent and kissed the older woman's cheek. 'Thora, Philippe said my name, he did, truly. And then he said "I am sorry" but I am sure I do not know what that means. Then he seemed to fall asleep . . . oh, Thora, I think I can hear the carriage wheels on the drive, it must be Mr Nesom. What a good man he is. Would you like to come up with me, Thora?'

But Thora shook her head. 'No, I cannot bring myself to see Philippe so ill, but I promise that I will come up if he asks for me.'

Mr Nesom was very satisfied with his patient. 'Miss Anna, I think he is past the worst. I have cupped him again and I expect him to sleep naturally now. That is nature's way of healing. He can have a little barley water today, but nothing to eat. If he continues well, you can give him some gruel in the morning, I will come sometime during the day. I think my diagnosis was correct for I have some more cases of influenza to visit today. You have done very well, Miss Anna.'

At Philippe's side again, Anna waited expectantly. But he slept for a long time and his tossing and turning ceased.

When he stirred, she propped him up on the pillows and he managed to drink a whole mugful of barley water.

'Anna,' he said quite clearly.

'Yes, Philippe, it is Anna. Would you like to see Thora?'

'No, not Thora, she is a good person, but I must tell Anna that I am sorry.'

Anna did not know quite what to do. 'Do not worry about that, Philippe. Look I am holding your hands, do you know me?'

'Anna,' he said clearly, and was asleep again.

The whole day passed in this fashion. He talked quite a lot but not so frantically. Anna found that she could understand a certain amount of what he said, but a lot of his words made no sense at all.

As it got dark, and Mrs Shapter lit the candles, Philippe seemed to look at the flickering light. Then he said quite clearly, 'Ah, it must be night-time. I will have a sleep now.'

Anna looked at Mrs Shapter and they both gave a chuckle. 'You would think he had not slept all day,' said Anna and there was some relief in her voice.

'He'll be all right now, miss, look he's breathing quite natural. Now you go and have a good sleep yourself. Shapter and I will manage between us. And you'd better go and tell Miss Peverill. A right worry she's been in, no mistake. I reckon she were scared he would die and her set on being mistress of Hatherley.'

Next morning, Mr Nesom pronounced his patient over the worst and he would not need to come again unles they sent for him. 'Plenty of good meat and some port wine to build him up again, Mrs Shapter, and you'll find him as fit as a fiddle in a couple of days.'

Mr Nesom was very accurate for two days later found Mr Philippe Peverill up and dressed and talking to Anna and Thora in the drawing-room.

'I have been very well nursed,' he said. 'I thank you both.'

Thora was honest and generous. 'Philippe, I confess that I am useless in a sick-room and all your thanks must go to Anna and the Shapters. Anna has been a heroine. I will leave you to thank her properly while I go to speak to Mrs Shapter about dinner.'

Anna watched Thora leave the room, then turned to Philippe. She was expecting him to be smiling but the Peverill frown was in his eyes.

'What is it, Philippe. Did you think it not proper that I should be sitting by your bedside on my own?'

'No, no, Anna, you were very kind. But you must tell me, it is imperative that I know: you say I was rambling in my fever and I want to know what I said to you. Did you make sense of anything?'

FIVE

There was a silence of several seconds and Anna did not know what to say. I do think he is afraid that he might have talked about his mistress, she said to herself.

Aloud, she stumbled over her words. 'I do not know what to say, Philippe. You see, for most of the time you were gabbling away in French and although I know some French, I could not understand a word . . . that is not quite true for I could pick out *Maman* and *Pierre*. Thora tells me that Pierre is your manservant.'

'And did I speak in English as well?' he asked with an edge to his voice.

Something bothers him, Anna thought, I must tell him the truth and put his mind at rest. 'Yes, you spoke in English but it was all nonsense. Some words you said again and again, but they were rubbish as though you were in a strange dream.'

'And they were?' he asked her sharply.

Whatever is it, wondered Anna? 'You kept talking about a door, and you had to carry something because you kept on and on about it. Then it sounded as though it was an evil thing . . . oh, and also knee, something about your knee, yet it didn't sound quite like knee, more like kneeve, which isn't even a word. I wondered if you had injured it so I told Mr Shapter; he was very good about bathing you and putting you into a clean nightshirt so that you would feel more comfortable. He told me that you had no injury to either knee.'

'I must thank them both,' Philippe said, and she noticed that his voice was a bit easier. 'And that was all?'

'That is all I can remember . . . oh no, there was salt, or something that sounded like salt. You kept saying it and I thought subconsciously you must have remembered that you should be given salt and water for a fever.'

'And I was given it?'

'Oh yes. I had Mrs Shapter prepare a saline draught as soon as I saw the state you were in.'

He leaned forward, took one of her hands and held it closely in both of his. 'How can I thank you, Anna? I am glad that I did not use any bad language, there is no knowing what will come out when one is delirious. It all sounds like a strange dream – or a nightmare – just as you say. What is it? You have thought of something else. You must tell me.'

'Yes, it was as you were improving a little. I would tell you that it was Anna and you would say my name quite clearly. But you kept saying "I must tell Anna I am sorry", or just "Anna, I am sorry". You had it on your mind that you must have hurt me in some way; I could not understand it.'

Philippe looked at her sensible face, the lovely grey eyes, the golden hair. What a practical, wonderful girl. It must have been on his mind that he had treated her as a young lady should not be treated.

'Have you forgotten the card-room at your come-out, Anna, and our ride up to Combe Down? I did not behave as a gentleman should and I must have had it on my conscience . . .' He looked at her confused expression. 'Or did you enjoy the kisses, Anna?'

Anna flushed scarlet. She had enjoyed the kisses, but she was not going to let this astonishing gentleman know it.

'You know that it was very wrong of you, Mr Peverill, on both occasions; it is no wonder that you had it on your conscience when you were in a fever. Perhaps you are not entirely bad if you wanted to apologize for your behaviour.'

'You have not revealed to me if the kisses pleased you. Shall I try again?'

'No, you will not, Mr Peverill, it is obvious that you are making a very swift recovery . . . no, you dare not.'

The last words were muffled, for he had leaned forward and touched her lips with his. It could hardly be called a kiss.

'I am not apologizing for that,' he said, looking into indignant eyes. 'It was very sweet; it was a thank you kiss.'

'I have done nothing, sir.'

'Yes, you have. You brought me back from a dark pit and you have given me a lot of amusement this morning though you are unaware of it. Perhaps I will be in a position to explain it to you one day.'

'You choose to be mysterious, Philippe,' she said stiffly.

'Ah, I am forgiven even if you do sound disapproving. You have called me by my name. Thank you, Anna.'

'You are incorrigible and I—' But Anna was stopped in mid-sentence by the return of Thora who immediately monopolized the conversation.

It took four weeks of cold, damp winter weather for Philippe to recover completely. Anna was soon back at Ponderfields, but she made many visits to Hatherley Park.

Now that Philippe was enjoying better health, Thora was fiercely possessive and Anna assumed that she was refasserting herself after Anna's control of the sick-room had stolen the care of her cousin from her.

By the end of February, spring still seemed distant in spite of the pussy willow to be found along the stream, but it was fine enough to go riding. Christopher came home for a week before the season of Lent was upon them. He could not persuade Anna to marry him but they remained good friends. During that week, the four of them twice rode up to Combe Down and Philippe seemed to change partners with no apparent effort on his behalf. He would gallop ahead with Anna, leaving Christopher to be gallant and accompany Thora.

On their first gallop and arrival at the trees at the top of the down, with Christopher and Thora not far behind, Anna remembered the embrace of the previous visit. She looked up at Philippe anxiously when she arrived at his side.

As before, he held out his arms to her.

'Do not dare to kiss me,' she said immediately. 'Thora is not far away.'

'I will kiss Thora as well, if you wish,' he replied, with a wicked grin.

'You are obviously quite recovered from your illness, Mr Peverill.'

'Jump, Anna. I will make a pact with you: I promise not to kiss you in front of Thora if you will come riding on your own with me when Christopher has returned to Battiscombe.'

'It is blackmail,' Anna declared, but she was laughing at the sudden and unusual roguishness of him.

'Would you like to come with me? Say yes quickly, they are almost upon us.'

'Yes,' she whispered, and knew herself for a fool.

'Good girl. . . .' and he turned quickly to greet Thora. 'Jump down, Thora, I will catch you.'

'I am quite able to dismount without help, Philippe,' said an ungracious Thora who was looking suspiciously at Anna. 'Are you flirting with Anna again? I noticed that the two of you soon galloped on ahead and arrived here first.'

'My dear Thora, why should I need to flirt with Anna when I have you? You know very well how much I value your friendship.' Anna heard his words and could guess that they were a charade on his part to keep the peace, and then Thora's reply showed that indeed he had succeeded in flattering his cousin. Something does not ring quite true, Anna thought.

'Philippe, I do know and I will not be jealous,' said Thora, looking pleased. 'It is lovely up here, is it not? The whole of Somerset stretched out around us and such a lovely view of Bath.'

While this exchange had been going on, Christopher had been speaking with Anna. He, too, had his suspicions. 'You are on very informal terms with Peverill, Anna,' he said to her. 'Have I cause for jealousy?'

Anna reached up and kissed his cheek. 'Of course not, Christopher. I am sorry I left you with Thora. Some little devil got into me and Corinna, she fled like the wind and I arrived here at the same time as Philippe. You have no reason to worry. First of all I have not promised to marry you, and then you must know that Thora is firmly attached to her cousin. I expect them to name the day at any time.'

'That remains to be seen, I think.' Christopher sounded sceptical and Anna laughed at him.

'You cannot imagine the two of them married to each other, can you?'

He shook his head. 'No, I cannot. Mr Philippe Peverill does not disappear for long stretches of time for no reason at all. Now, my Anna, tomorrow is my last day: what would you like to do?'

'You know what I would like to do, and we will not tell Philippe and Thora: I would like to go and look for primroses in the wood at Hatherley Park, just as we used to do when we were children.'

Christopher laughed. 'You are easily pleased, my dear. But I thought that Mr Peverill had warned you not to go into the wood.'

'He has proved to be not so haughty as we first thought him. I somehow think that his illness has mellowed him a little,' Anna said lightly.

'Very well then, I will ride over after breakfast and we will go primrosing, if that is what you wish.'

'Thank you . . . Christopher, you are such a nice person, do you know what I wish, though I am sure I have said it before?'

'What is it now, Miss Starkie?' he teased her.

'I wish you could meet a young lady in Battiscombe and fall head over heels in love with her. You could marry her and we would all be comfortable.' Anna smiled at him.

'And what about you, Anna?' he asked her.

'Perhaps I have yet to meet my destiny,' was her quick reply.

'I wonder,' said Christopher, but said no more. He had seen her expression sometimes when she was looking at Philippe Peverill. And even if that gentleman was attached to his cousin at the moment, there was something that was not quite right about the relationship at Hatherley Park.

The two of them enjoyed their walk in the wood and did manage to find some primroses hiding under the trees, then Christopher returned to his vicarage.

Philippe and Anna agreed to ride together the next day in the direction of Stanton Drew though they did not expect to reach the stone circle. He told her to meet him at the gates of Hatherley at ten o'clock.

The morning was misty but promised fine and Anna set off from Ponderfields on Corinna with a feeling of pleasant expectation. She loved the time of year, for the first green buds of the spring were showing on the trees and the air had lost its winter chill.

Her happy feelings were dashed when she saw Thora, also on horseback, at the gates of Hatherley Park. She seemed to be alone.

'Thora, is Philippe not well?' Anna asked anxiously.

'He has gone,' Thora replied bluntly.

'Gone?' Anna could only echo the word.

'Yes, I don't know why he should have made an assignation with you without telling me about it. As though I don't have enough trouble with his *affaire* and goings-on in Weymouth without him turning his eyes in your direction. I suppose it must be your youth, because you are not the prettiest of girls if you don't mind me saying so. Well, apart from all that, and because you and I have got on all right in the past, I have to tell you that Philippe received a messenger last night and he was away in the carriage at first light this morning. I don't know if the man was from London or Weymouth. As far as I'm concerned, London means business, Weymouth means pleasure and I don't have much say in the matter either way. So he tells me that he doesn't know how long he will be away and will I come to the gates at about ten o'clock and tell you what has happened and he is very sorry he had had to miss his ride with you.' Thora stopped to draw breath but Anna was speechless and let the angry woman carry on her tirade.

'All I can say is that it serves you right for having arranged to meet him in secret in the first place. You know very well that he is committed to me and has been for a long time now. It is my plan to be married before the year is out, then we can settle down at Hatherley Park. Well, I am sorry if I have carried on like this, but you can see that I am not very pleased at having been left on my own again. And I don't want to offend you because you are my only friend. Perhaps we can take up our walks and rides again as we did when Philippe was away before. Well, what have you to say for yourself?'

Anna was stunned, not only at Philippe's sudden disappearance, but at all the implications of Thora's tale of woe: she had never before mentioned that Philippe had a mistress in Weymouth. And it was now obvious that she was very much hurt by the circumstances of his libertine behaviour. He is as I first thought him, Anna said to herself, insufferably proud and careless of the feelings of those around him. I must try and put kind thoughts of him behind me and continue as a friend to Thora. For the first time she felt some pity for Philippe's cousin.

The other thing that occurred to her was the way in which Thora had spoken, and remembered she had thought Thora rather vulgar on their first meeting. Now she had spoken of Philippe in a way which did not quite become a lady. There is some mystery about Philippe, Anna thought, although that now seems to be explained by the mistress in Weymouth, but there is also a hint of mystery about Thora. However, it is no use me dwelling upon it; I must try and be friendly towards her as she is obviously so ill-used.

'Thora, I am sorry to hear all this. I know that there have been rumours in the village about Philippe, but I have turned a deaf ear to them. However, I can see that his behaviour has upset you and I am quite willing to go walking and riding with you as we did before.'

Thora smiled wanly. 'You are kind to show so much forbearance, Anna, and I thank you for your friendship. There is no knowing when we shall hear from Philippe again; I think he is best forgotten.'

Anna felt a dismal sinking of the heart, she would miss Philippe and their little altercations even though she knew he belonged to Thora – if that is indeed so, she thought. One begins to wonder.

And so April came and Eastertide with it and with no news from Philippe.

But the news from France had them all buzzing. On 6 April, Napoleon abdicated and was to be sent to Elba, and King Louis

XVIII returned to Paris. And the news from Lord Wellington and his redcoats, was that they were now marching to the capital from Toulouse.

It was a few days after Easter that Anna received her extraordinary message.

A carriage, which she later recognized as that of Philippe, arrived at Ponderfields. It was driven by a small, dark man who hurried round to the servants' quarters of the house.

Anna, as it happened, was in the library that morning, and was on her own when one of the maids came seeking her. 'Miss Anna, come quick. There is a Frenchman and he has a message for you. He has travelled from Weymouth so we are getting him some breakfast. But please come quick, Miss Anna.'

Anna was completely bewildered. The only word which made sense was Weymouth, for that place she always associated with Philippe. Could the message be from him? And what could he possibly want of her?

She hurried to the kitchen and indeed found a small, dark man of about forty years, drinking coffee.

He jumped up as soon as he saw her. 'You Miss Anna? I must see you pleez. Have important message.' He looked around him. 'But not here. My name is Pierre Leconte and I am the manservant of M. Philippe Peverill.'

Anna did not doubt him. There was sincerity as well as fear in his very dark eyes. 'Come into the library, Pierre, we can be private there.'

He followed her and she beckoned him into a chair at one side of the firepace; she sat opposite him trying to keep calm, but was inwardly alarmed at his unexpected arrival.

'It is to do with Mr Peverill?' she asked him. 'He is not ill again?'

'No, it is worse,' said Pierre.

'He is not dead?' she said, fearfully.

'No, not yet, but he is in danger,' was his reply.

'He is in Weymouth?' she asked next.

'No, he has not been in Weymouth for long time. He is in France; they have him in the town lock-up near Bayeux.'

Anna stared. Nothing was making sense.

'What is he doing in France?'

'It is his work,' said Pierre, as though that explained everything to her.

'But I thought he was in Weymouth to visit . . . it is not polite of me . . . to visit his mistress.'

Had Pierre looked less worried, she thought he would have chuckled. 'His *paramour*? *Non, non, non* – he goes to France to work for my Lord Wellington. *Ecoutez, s'il vous plaît*, he writes a letter to ask you to help him. You are Miss Anna? *Bon*, I have it here, you must read it carefully, it is very important.'

By this time, Anna thought that she must be going crazy. Philippe working for Lord Wellington? But he was not in the army. And in a lock-up in France? Nothing made sense. This Pierre was obviously Philippe's trusted manservant of many years. Thora had often spoken of him although Anna had never seen him at Hatherley. Now she must listen to him and do as he said.

He was holding out a rough piece of paper, it looked as though it had been torn out of the end of a book and the writing on it was in pencil. It was folded twice but not sealed. There were two words in capitals on the front: MISS ANNA.

With trembling fingers, she unfolded it and looked at the hastily written words; they were written in faint pencil but in a good hand.

My dear Anna

You are the only one I can ask and trust, please listen. I am in a lock-up near Bayeux. Because they heard me speaking English they think I am a spy.

Napoleon has abdicated, but in this village, the English are still the enemy. I have told them I have come to France to visit Maman in Paris, but they do not believe me. When I said that my wife in England would be worried because she had not received a letter telling her of my safe arrival, being ordinary country people they seemed to understand. Very well, they said, prove it. Bring your wife here and she will tell us the truth.

Anna, my dear Anna, will you travel to France with Pierre and pretend that you are my wife? They have not locked up Pierre because he is French, so they have allowed him to bring this note to my dear wife. They have not read it because they do not know any English.

I know I am asking the impossible but I believe that you can do it. Please try.

Your loving husband   Philippe

Anna must have looked stupefied for she heard Pierre say. 'Please, *mademoiselle.*'

'I must read it again, Pierre, it is difficult to make sense of it all. Will they really let Philippe go free if I can prove that I am his wife and tell them he is my husband and that he is not a spy. Is he a spy, Pierre?'

'*Oui, mademoiselle.*'

Anna swallowed hard and read the letter again, her thoughts were confused and chaotic. Philippe has not been visiting a mistress in Weymouth, or has he? He is in danger, he needs me. He knows that I can speak French. I will tell Mama I am going to Weymouth . . . my mind seems to be made up of its own accord, but what excuse can I give for going to Weymouth?

'*Mademoiselle?*' Pierre's voice trembled.

'Yes, I will do it, Pierre, but I must give a reason for going to Weymouth – I assume we would sail to France from there? What can I say?'

Pierre did not hesitate. 'Tell your mama that M. Philippe has a return of the fever. He is staying with his family in Weymouth – that has been true – and that he calls and calls for you. They are in fear of his life.'

She stared at him and then nodded. 'Yes, Mama knows that he did that the first time he had the fever. Pierre, I am crazy but I will do it. Go back to the kitchen and finish your breakfast. I will pack a small portmanteau and tell my mama. I will be at the carriage in half an hour.'

Anna left the library in haste, her head spinning. I am crazy, she said again, mad, foolhardy; I had best not stop to think or I will never do it. I must think of Philippe – she stopped. Philippe? I knew there was a mystery about him and now I know some of it. I must not hesitate – he who hesitates is lost, they say. I am coming, Philippe, I will not let you down. I promise to do my best.

Anna rushed into the drawing-room and was glad to find her mother on her own. She stopped at the door. I cannot tell her about going to France and about Philippe being imprisoned – it is not possible, I will do as Pierre suggested.

'Oh, Mama, I am glad that you are here. It is such bad news.'

'Whatever is it, my love?' Her mother looked anxious.

'I have had a visit from Mr Peverill's manservant, Pierre, and he tells me that Mr Peverill has had a return of that dreadful fever.'

'But I thought that Mr Peverill was away from home.'

'Yes, he is in Weymouth.'

'But, Anna, it is well known in the village why he goes to Weymouth. How can it possibly concern you?' Her mother's voice was raised.

'He calls for me, Mama, he did before if you remember.'

'And I never knew why,' was the abrupt reply.

Anna ignored this remark. 'Pierre says that his family have asked if I will go. And you know that I have never taken any notice of village gossip.'

THE PROUD MR PEVERILL

'Anna, you cannot go to Weymouth on your own, even if Mr Peverill is very ill.'

'But I will have Pierre; he has driven the carriage here.'

'But Pierre is only the manservant.' Her mother's voice was rising and rising.

Anna was frantic; would her mother never understand? 'Mama, I know from Thora that Pierre has been with Mr Peverill for years and years, everything is entrusted to him. Yes, I know he is French, but he is very capable and it is not as though I would be travelling alongside him; I will be inside the carriage.'

'But you must have a maid with you, dear.'

'I do not need a maid, Mama, it is not as though I am travelling on the common stage. And it is only the next county. You make it sound as though I am going to strangers at the other side of the country.'

'Anna, you are being disrespectful to me.'

Anna sighed; her mother was refusing to even try and understand. I will have to try again. 'Mama, I must go if it will help the Peverills. I would never forgive myself if Mr Peverill did not recover and I had refused to go to him.'

'But I still do not understand why it must be you, Anna. Why is he not asking for his cousin? She should be the person to go.'

Anna shook her head. 'I am afraid Thora has a dread of the sickroom; it was all left to me, last time. And the Shapters, of course. You are a kind person, Mama, and I believe I have that same kindness in me.'

Mrs Starkie spoke more gently. 'The kindness is all on your side, Anna. Look how comfortable you have made us since you received your legacy. I suppose I cannot stop you. I must look upon it as an act of mercy even if you are going off with some unknown Frenchman.'

'Mama' Anna was losing her patience. 'He is not unknown to

me and if you would like to judge for yourself and it would make you happier, please go and talk to Pierre. He is in the kitchen. He drove up from Weymouth before breakfast and Cook is giving him something to eat.'

As Mrs Starkie rose from her chair, Anna had another thought. 'Mama, I have not time to see Miss Peverill before I go, so if she comes to enquire after me, please will you tell a little lie and say I have gone to relatives in Bath?'

'But that is a shocking lie, Anna, not a little one. Whatever has come over you?'

'No, it is not shocking, it is a kindness. I do not want to worry Thora, you remember how badly she took it when Philippe was ill last time.'

Mrs Starkie paused at the door. 'You call him Philippe, Anna, that appears to be excessively familiar.'

'Thora always calls him Philippe. He is her cousin and they are going to be married after all.' Anna felt snappish. 'Now I will go and pack my bag. You go and talk to Pierre and I am sure you will come to agree with me.'

'Very well, Anna, if you say so,' said Mrs Starkie, stiffly, and marched off to the kitchen.

When Anna came downstairs with her portmanteau, she found her mother at the foot of the stairs and she was smiling. There was no sign of Pierre.

'A very polite and respectable gentleman, this Pierre, even if he is French. I do not wonder that Mr Peverill has kept him all these years. You will be safe with him, Anna, and he will bring you home again as soon as Mr Peverill has made a recover. I do believe that you are doing the right thing and I will ignore any improprieties in it. The Peverills are a good family. I trust that you will have a safe and swift journey, Anna. Please give my best wishes to poor Mr Peverill.'

Anna kissed her mother and hurried out of the house. There she saw Philippe's carriage with Pierre waiting for her. He gave a grin as he took her portmanteau.

'Your mama was in a worry, yes? I speak to her the best I could, Miss Anna.'

Anna thanked him. 'You did very well, Pierre, she was much happier after she had spoken to you. Thank you.' She paused before she let him help her into the carriage. 'How long will it take us, Pierre?'

'I have put fresh horses on, Miss Anna, and we will not need a change, just a stop for some food, maybe at Ilchester. It is fifty miles. We will be in Weymouth by the middle of the afternoon. You leave it all to me, *mademoiselle*.'

And Anna did just that. She sat in the coach, hardly glancing as the Somerset countryside passed her by. She was clutching Philippe's note and before they had reached Weymouth, she must have read it a hundred times. They were on turnpike roads all the way and made good progress. Part of it was the old Fosse Way, the Roman Road from Lincoln to Exeter and even the towns they passed through – Ilchester, Dorchester – echoed their Roman origins.

The break at the small town of Ilchester was very welcome even though Anna felt uncomfortable because she was travelling without a maid. However, she put on a haughty voice – which she thought would please Philippe – and asked for a private room, and some cold meat and small ale.

Soon they were in Dorset, and after drinking the ale, Anna dozed for a short while. Then she was wide awake as they passed through Dorchester and she knew that they would shortly be in Weymouth.

She read Philippe's letter for the last time and put it in her reticule. It was no use trying to make sense of what Pierre had told her, but the questions kept posing themselves. If Philippe was a spy for Lord Wellington, why had he come to Hatherley Park? Did Thora know of his activites when he was away? It would seem not as Thora had hinted that indeed he did visit his mistress in Weymouth. And who was she going to find in Weymouth? A kept woman? Or maybe he simply had a lodging which he used before crossing to France.... Stop it, Anna, she told herself. You must be single-minded and not dwell on all these possibilities. You will know some of the truth very shortly.

Weymouth at last and Pierre stopped outside a neat house, which was one of a row of houses built in the style of fifty years earlier.

Pierre opened the carriage door and smiled. 'We are here, Miss Anna. Let me take you in before I take the horses round to the stables.'

Anna was feeling nervous, but there was no place for nerves in this exercise, she thought quickly.

A maid opened the door at Pierre's knock, and he asked her to take Miss Starkie to her mistress.

At the drawing-room door, Anna heard the announcement. 'Miss Caroline, here is Miss Anna Starkie for you.'

Anna stepped into the room. Standing before her was a girl whom she thought could not be more than eighteen years of age. Petite would describe her, thought Anna, as she gazed speechless, for this *Miss Caroline* was small, dark and slim and very, very pretty.

This was Philippe's mistress? she was asking herself, with a sick horror. She found she had no words.

SIX

THE YOUNG LADY in front of Anna spoke softly and her eyes had a slight frown. 'Miss Starkie? I am so pleased that you have come, but there is something bothering you. Does it worry you that Papa has asked you to this for him? You are not much more than my age and Papa has asked you to pretend to be his wife . . . why, what is it?'

'Papa?' Anna could only manage the one word.

'Yes, Papa. He is in prison in France. They will let him go if he can prove that he is not a spy, just a gentleman travelling to Paris. But you know all this – Pierre let me read your letter from Papa.'

Anna was trying to grasp what must be the correct facts. 'Tell me quickly, the person you call Papa, is he Mr Philippe Peverill?'

'Of course he is . . . why are you laughing? There is nothing to laugh at today, I can assure you.'

For Anna had exploded into gasps of mirth. 'You are Philippe's daughter?'

'Of course I am, who did you think I was?'

'I thought you were his mistress,' Anna blurted out.

'His mistress? Oh, goodness gracious me,' and the young lady who was Caroline Peverill burst into laughter along with Anna.

Then she recovered and spoke seriously. 'Now we must stop laughing and introduce ourselves properly. I am Miss Caroline Peverill, the only daughter of Mr Philippe Peverill – my mother died when I was born, and my aunt brought me up. We are in such terrible trouble today. But now you have arrived. Papa likes you, I know he does, for he said in the letter that you were the only person he could trust. You had better call me Caroline and I will call you Anna . . . oh, here is Pierre.'

She stopped in mid-sentence as Pierre entered the room. He had washed and neatened himself after the journey.

'Miss Caroline, what is this I have heard from Cook, eh?'

And for a reply, Anna watched in astonishment as Caroline threw herself into his arms and burst into tears. I am going crazy and not for the first time today, she thought, as she watched the Frenchman hold on to the sobbing Caroline, patting her dark curls. *'Ma petite, ma petite,'* he kept saying.

Anna's thoughts were in a whirl. First of all, Philippe does not have a mistress but a young daughter, and now his daughter throws herself into a servant's arms as though he was a lover. She was thankful when Caroline turned from Pierre to speak to her.

'Anna, you must think it strange that Pierre comforts me, but you see, he is like a very favourite uncle to me. He has taken care of me ever since I was born. We have had bad news today after Pierre left to come to you, so we are in even greater trouble than before.'

Pierre turned to Anna. 'Miss Anna, you must listen to what Miss Caroline has to say for we are *at a pass*, I think you say, and we all need to talk together. I will go to the kitchen to fetch a tray of tea from Cook and Miss Caroline will tell you of the further calamity which has fallen upon us.'

Anna did sit down and Caroline sat near her. 'I can tell that I am going to like you for you have not hesitated about going to rescue

Papa. I am sorry that you were led to believe that I was his mistress. You mean he has never told you that he has a daughter? Why is that?'

Anna found her tongue at last. 'He has always been very secretive about where he goes when he leaves Hatherley Park, and there has been a lot of gossip about him having a mistress in Weymouth. Then his cousin led me to believe that the stories were true—' she was interrupted.

'Thora? Bah, she lets it be known that she is going to marry Papa, but I do not wish to have her for a stepmother. I did not even know that we had a distant Peverill cousin until Thora came.'

'I doubt that Philippe will marry her, Caroline.'

'I hope that you are right . . . perhaps he will marry you if you pretend to be his wife.'

Anna laughed. 'We will see how that goes, but what is it that has happened to upset you today?'

'I will tell you as we drink our tea – here is Pierre with the tray. Pierre is like one of the family, Anna.'

'Very well,' replied Anna. These Peverills are full of surprises, she told herself, wondering what she was going to hear next.

'Thank you, Pierre, I will tell Anna about Tante Michelle, and then we must discuss what to do for the best.' The young girl turned to Anna.

'My mama died when I was born, as I told you, and I was placed with Papa's older sister, Michelle, who had never married. To understand us, you must know that there were four Peverill children; Michelle, the eldest, then Jean-Luc, he died when he was a little boy, then came Marie and lastly Philippe. Papa is the youngest. You will notice that they were all given French names. Did you know that my *grandmère* is French?'

Anna nodded, feeling on safer ground. 'Yes, Philippe told me.'

'I am glad you call him Philippe, that makes it easier. So, as I said, I was brought up by my aunt and I call her Tante Michelle; she is the best mother a girl could ever have.'

'Where is she, Caroline?' asked Anna thinking that this must be the problem.

'I will tell you, for it all happened today. What a day! First of all, Pierre leaves before it is even light to take Papa's letter to you and hopefully, to bring you back. Tante Michelle was certain from what Papa had said of you that you would not refuse. And then a letter came with the morning mail and it was bad news. My other aunt, Marie, was very ill and would Philippe and Michelle go to London immediately. Poor Tante Michelle, she did not know what to do; she must go to London, but how could she leave me alone here when she knew that Pierre would probably be off to France with you tomorrow? "I must find someone to stay with you", she said to me, "perhaps Mrs Belcher would come". I will tell you about Mrs Belcher in a minute. But I made her go; I was sure you would come, Anna, and between us we would be able to think of something if Mrs Belcher could not come for any reason.'

Caroline paused and looked at Anna anxiously. 'Do you understand all that? I am sorry it is so complicated. Everything seems to have happened at once: Papa in prison; you coming to rescue him; Tante Marie ill, and Tante Michelle going to her in London. She went on the first stagecoach, for I insisted on it, and here I am left on my own in Weymouth.'

Anna was trying to take it all in. 'You cannot stay here on your own, Caroline, you are too young to be without a chaperon.' She was thinking hard, looking at Pierre. 'Could you stop with Caroline, Pierre, and I will go to France on my own?'

Pierre looked shocked. 'Miss Anna, it would not be safe for you to be on your own. You could cross to Cherbourg on the *Marie-Rose* for Captain Hart would take care of you, but you would need an escort to Bayeux. I must arrange all that and take you to *monsieur*.'

Anna looked at Caroline. 'You must have made friends in Weymouth, Caroline, is there no one who would come to you, or you could go to them? Who is this Mrs Belcher?'

Caroline shook her head. 'She is our neighbour and she is a very good person but that is another story. We have not made ourselves known to anyone; you see, Papa's work is very secret. Pierre knows and I know, but that is all. We have not made friends with anyone but it does not worry me for I have always had *ma chère tante* here, and in between, Pierre and Papa would come. Even you did not know that Papa had a daughter. One day, I will laugh about it all, with you thinking I was Papa's *chère-amie*, but not today.'

Anna had the instinctive feeling that she could grow to love Caroline very quickly. There is something very French about her, she thought, but that is not surprising. Whatever can I think of? And suddenly she wished she had Christopher there to help her; he could always get them out of tangles such as this. And she sat up with a start, with an astonishing vision of Christopher and Caroline together; he would adore her, she was telling herself furiously, I must try to do some match-making. But that is in the future; you must think, Anna, and think quickly.

She looked at Caroline. 'There is one thing I do not understand, and that is why your Tante Michelle went off in such a rush this morning and left you all on your own. She sounds such a caring sort of person that I cannot imagine why she should do such a thing. Is it something to do with this Mrs Belcher? You were going to tell me.'

'Tante Michelle is very caring, and it was not her fault, for she made the arrangements before she left for the stage. She sent Dorcas – who is my maid – round to Mrs Belcher next door, but

Dorcas was so long fetching her that Tante Michelle had to hurry off. She had no doubts that Mrs Belcher would come as she is the one good friend we have, but even Mrs Belcher does not know about Papa. Tante Michelle thought that she was just setting her house in order and putting some things she might need into a bag, so she went off for the stage without any hesitation.'

'And what went wrong with the arrangment?' asked Anna gently. The girl seemed distressed that her Tante Michelle might be blamed.

'Dorcas discovered that Mrs Belcher had gone to her daughter's house near the harbour. So Dorcas went after her, only to find that Mrs Belcher was badly needed at Ellen's because her baby was arriving early ... oh, it was all such a muddle, but the upshot was that Dorcas came back to me and said that Mrs Belcher could not come.'

'So what did you do?'

'Dorcas and I talked about it and we decided to wait and see what Pierre said when he brought you here.'

'You were sure that he would bring me?' asked Anna.

'Yes.' The one word was very decisive.

'Why was that?'

Caroline smiled for the first time. 'Papa has spoken of you in such a way that I knew that he liked you especially. So I wanted to meet this Anna and I had a feeling you would come and you did.' She paused and looked at the older girl. 'But, Anna, before I started telling you about Mrs Belcher, I thought you looked as though you had thought of something to help us out of our predicament.'

Anna nodded. 'Yes, something has come to me. But let me try and work it out.' And words connected themselves in her mind – Caroline, Christopher, Mrs Boyd, stagecoach, rectory, Mama.

'Is it helpful?' asked Caroline.

'I am not sure; it would mean a great deal of courage on your part.'

'I have a lot of courage,' said Caroline proudly, reminding Anna of Philippe.

'Caroline, I will speak slowly and you listen, too, Pierre. My mama would be pleased to have you to stay at Ponderfields, Caroline, but you would have to travel there on the stagecoach for Pierre will not be here to drive the carriage. I know that there is a stage between Weymouth and Bath, but it does not go past Ponderfields and there would be no one to meet you. But the stage does go past the rectory, and the Reverend and Mrs Boyd are our dearest friends. If you could be brave enough to travel on the stagecoach – you would have to take your maid with you – we can ask the coachman to put you off at the rectory in West Wilton. He will know. And I will write a note to Mrs Boyd and ask her to take you to my mama.'

Caroline was staring at Anna, Pierre was smiling. 'You are very clever, Anna,' said the young girl.

'No, not clever, just sensible. What do you think of the idea? Could you do it, and would your maid go with you?'

Caroline smiled. 'I *will* do it, it will be an adventure. Why should Papa have all the adventures while I sit at home? And it will solve all our problems and you and Pierre can go off to rescue Papa without having to worry about me. And, yes, Dorcas is my very own lady's maid and before that she was my nursery-maid. She will take care of me. And I will enjoy it on the stagecoach. What do you say to the plan, Pierre?' she asked, turning to him. He had been following the conversation intently.

He was all smiles. '*Bien. Bien.* You will be quite safe with Madame Starkie; she is a good lady. I speak with her this morning, she will take care of you until our return. And now it is my turn to speak of our plans, so please listen. I will now go and get two tickets for the stagecoach to Bath for first thing tomorrow morning. Miss Anna and I will see you safely away, Miss Caroline, and then....' he turned to Anna. 'Miss Anna, we will walk to the harbour where the *Marie-Rose* is waiting and cross over to France. When we all return, we will bring the carriage to West Wilton for you.' He got up. 'I will go now and leave you two *mademoiselles* to have the coze, I think you say.'

Anna sank back in her chair and looked at Caroline who was more at ease than she had been on Anna's arrival.

'I do not know how I will ever thank you, Anna,' said the younger girl. 'Everything is so complicated, I hardly know where to start with my gratitude. Your mama will not mind me staying at your house until Papa comes? But surely she does not know why you have come here? Did you have to invent a story?'

Anna looked rueful. 'Caroline, I have never been caught up in so many inventions in all my life.'

'How old are you, Anna? I am eighteen.'

'I am twenty and I have a big secret which only Mama knows, but I hope to tell you about it one day. I am sorry if I thought you were Philippe's mistress, but it was really his fault for not telling us that he had a daughter.'

'It was funny, Anna,' said Caroline, still smiling at the mistake.

'Do you know,' Anna thought suddenly. 'I have just remembered that Thora told me that Philippe had been made a widower when he was a young gentleman, but she made no mention of a daughter. How much does Thora know?'

'She knows everything.'

'Oh dear,' sighed Anna.

'What is it?' asked Caroline. 'How have you explained your journey to Weymouth? You cannot have told the truth.'

'Caroline, my mama thinks that I have come to Weymouth because your papa is ill with fever again and that he is asking for me. He is supposed to be with his family which, fortunately, has proved to be true. Not only that, I have told Mama that if Thora asks after me, Mama is to say that I am visiting relatives in Bath. . . .' She stopped for she could see that Caroline had a hand to her mouth to stop herself from laughing. 'Do not dare to laugh at me, young Caroline. Do you realize that I have to tell more lies to persuade my mama to look after you at Ponderfields?'

'Anna, I am sorry. It is a real scrape, is it not? Will you give me a letter for your mama? Whatever will you say?'

Anna was thoughtful. 'I think it will have to be more lies, for Mama already thinks that Philippe is lying very ill here. Let us write the letter together, Caroline can you get some paper and pen and ink?'

'We will go into the library and sit at Papa's desk,' said Caroline immediately.

Anna sat at Philippe's desk thinking hard. What a terrible tangle I am in, she thought, and it seems that one lie leads to another until we are caught up in a web of lies of our own making.

'I will say the words aloud as I write them,' she told Caroline. 'But you must stop me if you think it is wrong.'

'Yes, I will.' Caroline had become serious.

My dear Mama

I am glad that I have come to Weymouth as they were very pleased to see me. All the gossips of West Wilton were wrong, for Mr Peverill's family is here and he has a young daughter, Caroline, who is eighteen years of age. Caroline's mother died when she was born and she has been brought up by an aunt. I fear that Caroline will catch the fever, so I will share the nursing with her aunt. I do not worry about myself for I did not catch it last time.

So I am writing to ask you, dear Mama, if you would keep Caroline safely at Ponderfields until Mr Peverill is well enough to travel? I shall be happier if I know she is safely with you and you will enjoy her company. She is a sweet child.

She is going to travel on the stage with her maid, Dorcas, who is very capable. We will need the carriage here. As the stage passes the rectory, she is to be set down there and the Boyds will bring her to you. I have written a note to Mrs Boyd.

Thank you, dear Mama

Your loving daughter Anna

Anna put the pen back on the standish and looked at Caroline.

'You did not stop me once,' she said, and found that Caroline was looking at her with some admiration.

'But you made it all sound true, I could never have written such a clever and loving letter.

Anna grinned. 'I must be a schemer by nature,' she replied. 'I have never told so many falsehoods. You are quite happy with what I said? And will you be able to keep up the fable of your papa's illness once you are at Ponderfields?'

Caroline nodded. 'I will try very hard.'

'I am sure you will succeed,' said Anna. 'Now, a short note to Mrs Boyd. This will be easier.'

Dear Mrs Boyd

I think Mama will have told you that I am in Weymouth with the Peverill family because Mr Peverill has a return of the fever. I am sending his daughter, Caroline, to stay at Ponderfields with Mama until we return. As the stage does not pass Ponderfields, I am asking the coachman to set Caroline down at the rectory. So I hope that I am not imposing upon you too much to ask you to take Caroline to Mama.

With thanks and kindest regards

Anna

Post scriptum: I think Caroline might do for Christopher!

'Anna,' exploded Caroline. 'What is that post scriptum? Whatever do you mean by it?'

Anna chuckled. 'It is a tease. One day you will discover the meaning for yourself. I will tell you no more.'

'It is you who is a tease,' said Caroline. 'But I will be patient because you are so good to me. And now I must find Dorcas and she will pack our portmanteaux, then we will have dinner and—'

Anna interrupted. 'And I hope you will tell me the truth about your papa.'

'I will tell you as much as I know, but I am afraid that it is very little.'

After dinner, they sat round the fire in the drawing-room; it seemed that the pair of them would never run out of things to say to each other.

Caroline's main worry seemed to be Anna's venture into France. 'Anna, do you really have the courage to go to the prison and try and set Papa free?'

Anna shook her head. 'I don't know. I seem to be caught in a plot of my own making. I could have refused Philippe and I suppose that any sensible girl would have done so; but there was something telling me that I could not let him down.' She stopped and looked at Philippe's daughter. 'All this has been a great shock to me. I guessed that there was some mystery about Philippe because of his association with Weymouth and all the gossip that went on about him. We became accustomed to him being away for long periods. Eventually, Thora and I became friends. You do not seem to like her but she is loyal to Philippe, and if she is Philippe's cousin then she must be your cousin, too.'

Caroline remained silent and Anna had the feeling that here was another piece of the mystery, it was almost like a difficult jigsaw. She kept finding the pieces but could not put them together. She went on speaking.

'But not one of us guessed that he was acting as a spy for Lord Wellington. We have followed the Peninsular War with great interest, as it so happens that the Boyds' eldest son, John, is a redcoat and was with Lord Wellington at Salamanca and Talavera. The last news we had was that they had spent a miserable winter encamped in the Pyrenees and that in the spring, Lord Wellington hoped to push Marshal Soult and the French Army back into France. But I believe from the daily paper that Lord Wellington is already on the way to Paris. Is that where your papa was heading for?'

Caroline shook her head. 'I have had no news. Usually he sends letters, but this time, nothing. He has been gone for more than a month and we, too, have heard of the advance to Paris, also that Napoleon has abdicated.' She paused. 'You must realize, my dear Anna, that I am used to this. When Papa first entered the service of Sir Arthur Wellesley, as he was then, I was quite small and could not understand what it was all about. We moved to this nice house in Weymouth and Papa would come and go and Pierre with him. I did not even have a governess it was all so secret, but Tante Michelle made up for that.' She stopped speaking and seemed lost in thought.

'What is it, Caroline? Something worries you?'

'It is something I never really understood. It was this strange move to Hatherley Park, all in secret; even I do not know the whole of it so I cannot tell you. I did not like Thora, especially when she started casting her eyes in Papa's direction. He brought her to Weymouth but I did not go to Hatherley and no one in West Wilton knew that I was here. I did not mind, for when Papa was home, we would have fine times together. He is a good father and I think he must be a good spy for this is the first time he has got himself caught. And it seems so strange that he should go through all the war with Napoleon almost unharmed and then get caught just as we hope that peace will come.'

She looked at Anna. 'I am sorry, I have gone on and on, but I think it will help you if you know all about it. And, please Anna, you will bring him safely home, won't you. . . ?' Her voice faltered and Anna saw the tears trickling down her cheeks.

Anna went to her then and knelt at the young girl's side, she took a handkerchief and wiped away the tears. Then she kissed Caroline's cheek. 'You are older than your years, my dear, and you are very loyal to your papa. I promise that I will do my very best to release him from the jail and bring him home. You go off to West Wilton tomorrow and enjoy yourself with my mama. Oh, I forgot to tell you that I have three young sisters who are still in the schoolroom. Now you must smile because I am going to tell you an amusing story about your papa's behaviour on the day of my come-out in Bath.'

'You have only just made your come-out, Anna?'

'Yes, but that is another story and will have to wait until all these excitements are over and we are all safely together again.'

'What were you going to tell me about Papa?'

So the story of Philippe's appearance at the Upper Rooms in Bath in all his dirt was told; and how he had wickedly taken her on one side in the card-room, which was quite improper – but the occasion of the stolen kiss was omitted from the tale.

Caroline clapped her hands. 'That is just like Papa, he will marry you, Anna, and you will be my stepmama and we will all live happily ever after. It is like a fairy-tale.'

'I cannot be your stepmama, Caroline, I am only two years older than you,' Anna reminded her.

'I had not thought of that. Do you think it matters?'

Anna laughed. 'We really are getting into the realms of fancy now. I think we must be more practical and have an early night for there will be a lot to think about in the morning.'

It was all a rush the following morning. Anna was pleased to find that Dorcas was a pleasant, sensible woman of over thirty years of age, who was obviously devoted to Caroline. Pierre took them all to the coaching inn and Caroline and Dorcas boarded the waiting stagecoach and took their places. They were travelling inside so would not suffer if there happened to be rain during the journey; their luggage was safely stowed away outside.

Caroline had kissed Anna goodbye and had whispered, 'Thank you for coming, Anna. I will be thinking of you and I hope that the next time I see you, that you will have Papa with you.'

Back at the house, Pierre told Anna of the arrangements he had made. 'I will have to leave the carrriage here, Miss Anna. Do you think you can walk as far as the harbour? We will possibly stay two or three nights in France, so you will need only a small bag which I will carry for you.'

Anna felt more positive and single-minded about her mission now that she had succeeded in sending Caroline off to West Wilton.

'Yes, Pierre, I am accustomed to long walks in the country and I have my half-boots with me. Tell me something about the sailing yacht which is going to take us to France. Do you know, I have never been to sea before. Is it Mr Peverill's own ship?'

'No, it is not, Miss Anna. It is a Revenue Cutter belonging to the government. You know what a Revenue Cutter is?'

She nodded. 'Yes, I believe I do. Is it not the sailing vessel which is out to catch the smugglers coming over from France?' And suddenly, there came to Anna the remembrance that one of the rumours about Philippe was that he was involved in smuggling. It is no wonder, she smiled inwardly, if he is associated with the Revenue Cutters.

'That is correct, Miss Anna. M. Philippe, he always uses the same cutter and the master of the ship is Captain Hart who will look after you. I do not suppose that you know if you suffer from the *mal-de-mer* as we call it?'

Anna laughed. 'I sincerely hope not, Pierre, but I will have you to look after me.'

'*Oui, mademoiselle*, I look after you just as I do Miss Caroline for you are very good and very brave to perform such a task to rescue M. Philippe.'

'I will do my best. I will now go and put some things in a bandbox for the journey.'

By the time Anna was walking at Pierre's side to the harbour, she had a feeling of excitement. Weymouth had been a very popular resort with King George and Queen Charlotte before the king's illness, and even that day in early spring, the town and harbour were busy. Anna found it thrilling to see the sea for the first time in her life, and was astonished at the number of sailing vessels in the harbour.

A thought struck her and she looked up at Pierre. 'Does Captain Hart know where we are going and why, Pierre?'

He looked at her seriously. 'Captain Hart has his instructions. He is told by the Foreign Office who he takes to France and when to bring them back. He obeys his commands and asks no questions; the rest is secret though I think it will puzzle him why we take a young lady with us this time.'

SEVEN

ANNA WAS SHOWN over the cutter by Captain Hart before they set sail and she found it very interesting; if he was mystified because he had been asked to carry a young lady to Cherbourg, he showed no sign of curiosity and was extremely polite. He took little notice of Pierre whom he seemed to know well.

The crossing of the English Channel took several hours and Anna enjoyed the new experience; she was never alone for when Captain Hart was needed elsewhere, she found Pierre by her side. She did not feel in the least sickly, indeed she enjoyed a hearty luncheon, sharing a table with the captain.

The sea was not entirely calm for there was a fresh breeze and it filled the white sails and speeded them on their way. Anna was fascinated by the swathe cut through the grey waters of the English Channel by the cutter and by the white foam left in its wake. The crew hurried about their tasks and she knew that she was fortunate in having an easy crossing.

Some of the time her thoughts were occupied with what lay ahead of her, but as she had little idea what to expect, she dismissed the tiny fears as foolish.

When they were within half an hour of the north coast of France, she found Pierre once more by her side. 'We must speak,

Miss Anna,' he said quietly. 'I have left you to enjoy your first travel on the sea, but now you must know something of our arrangements.'

'Yes, Pierre, I thought you would soon be telling me.'

'M. Philippe has a small house in Cherbourg which he has used for many years. It is kept ready for him by M. and Mme. Barnard. M. Barnard is English and married a French lady many years ago; their children are now grown up and have left home. They know a little about M. Philippe but not all. It was necessary for me to tell them of *monsieur*'s imprisonment and the plan we had made. So they are expecting you, Miss Anna, and you will find them kind and discreet. They will give us a dinner tonight and we will sleep there; it is all quite proper, I think you say.'

'And when do we go to Mr Peverill, Pierre?'

'*Un moment, mademoiselle*. First of all, I will have to go and seek a conveyance which will take us both; before I was on horseback but that will not do. So in the evening, I will find a small cart which will take the three of us for we hope to have *monsieur* with us on our return, *n'est-ce pas*? We will set off first thing tomorrow morning.'

'It is easier for you because you are French. I will try to speak in French if I can.'

'It will not be necessary in the home of M. Barnard as they both speak English and French equally well, you will find. When we reach Florennes, that is the village where *monsieur* is held, we will speak as necessary. But that is enough. You understand, Miss Anna?'

'Yes, thank you for explaining it all to me, Pierre, it does help me, but I think that I will be feeling a little nervous tomorrow morning.'

'Pah,' was the reply from Pierre. 'You have the courage, Miss Anna, or you would not be here.'

'I hope so,' she said, and tried not to think too far ahead.

Her reception at the Barnard's cottage was a happy affair; she was shown a small room on the first floor and made to feel welcome and comfortable.

Neither husband nor wife asked her why she had come, and their talk was mainly of their family. And as she was able to talk about Mrs Starkie and her sisters, they spent a pleasant evening. Pierre was out somewhere in the town and Philippe was not mentioned; Anna went to bed hoping that she would sleep and not let her mind dwell on unforeseen difficulties.

As she undressed in the small room, she thought that the hours spent in the fresh sea air must have tired her, for she kept yawning and then slept well.

She was woken by a smiling Mme. Barnard who had brought some warm water for washing and a cup of hot chocolate.

'*Merci, madame,*' Anna said with a sleepy smile.

'*Vous avez le courage, ma fille,*' said Mme. Barnard, the only reference that was made to the venture ahead.

Pierre was pleased when she came downstairs in good time; she was dressed in the same clothes as on the previous day, a deep-blue dress of a heavy cotton, unfashionably high to the neck but serving its purpose.

'Miss Anna, you must eat a good breakfast. Madame has the fresh croissants and some ham. I have found a conveyance for us which I think will serve; it needs only the one horse and hopefully will seat the three of us.'

'You will help me, Pierre?' she asked him, and it was her only sign of faltering.

'I will be with you all the time, Miss Anna, do not fear.'

They breakfasted, made their farewells and Anna went upstairs for her pelisse and bonnet. Outside, Pierre had the cart ready at the door and a patient grey waiting to take them to Bayeux. Anna thought it looked like what in England would have been called a gig, but it was slightly larger and there was certainly room for two passengers alongside the driver.

Pierre helped her up but before he started off, he turned to her and held out something in his hand.

'Miss Anna, you must wear this. It is *monsieur*'s signet ring and it will be too big for you, but please to place it on your wedding finger. Your left hand, Miss Anna, the fourth finger.'

Anna did not say a word but took the ring and put it on her finger as directed. It was too big, but she thought that if she kept her fingers closed up then it would not look so loose.

'*Ça va*, Miss Anna?'

'Yes, thank you, Pierre, I would not have thought of it,' she replied and waved goodbye to M. and Mme. Barnard.

It was as they left the cheerful couple, that Anna suddenly felt terrified. They were driving towards the outskirts of the busy port of Cherbourg, but Anna saw nothing of the French town.

'Pierre?' she cried, her hand on his arm. 'I cannot do it.'

He glanced down at her white face and drove more slowly. 'Miss Anna, please think of all the times that you have seen M. Philippe. Remember him. Ask yourself why it is you that he has asked to do this for him. He could have asked for Miss Thora, but he did not. It is you he wants and only you will know why.'

And Anna was back in England, seeing the haughty Mr Peverill in the wood; seeing the travel-stained Philippe at her come-out, daring to kiss her; remembering their rides up to Combe Down and another kiss; and last of all, remembering the feverish Philippe who had called only for herself and now he had called for her again and she must be there.

She looked up at Pierre. 'I will go, Pierre. Tell me about the journey so that I will have something else to think about; the countryside looks very flat and uninteresting.'

'It is the Cherbourg Peninsula, Miss Anna, and almost surrounded by the sea, so it is flat everywhere. Soon we will reach the village of Valognes, and then Ste-Mère-Église, that is a nice name, *n'est-ce pas*? Then Carentan, and we will be on the road to Bayeux, but we do not go as far as that historic town. You know of the famous tapestry? And all the time we are on the road to Paris which is not so far away. It is where M. Philippe was hoping to go and try to see his *maman* – his mother, I should say – but the disaster overtook him when we stopped in the village of Florennes. We were speaking to each other in English and the gendarme happened to hear us and nothing that I could say would convince them that M. Philippe was not an English spy.'

'But they did not take you, Pierre?'

'*Oui*, they did take me, but when *monsieur* insisted that his wife would speak for him, they let me bring the letter and you know the rest, Miss Anna. But do not fear, they are village people and we will soon convince them.'

'But Philippe *is* a spy.'

'Hush, Miss Anna, it is not safe. We will talk in French now if it is not too difficult for you.'

'*Certainement*, Pierre' she said, and managed a smile. Florennes was a large village and had a gendarmerie in the main square. Pierre pulled up outside and helped Anna down. She saw, with some nervousness, that there was an armed guard standing outside, a tall man in uniform and holding a rifle.

'Say nothing,' said Pierre in French to her and they approached the guard.

'You have M. Peverill here?' asked Pierre, and Anna thought that he spoke in a voice of authority which she would never have dreamed he possessed for he was always kind and gentle with her.

'Yes, he is here. What do you want with him?' asked the guard and Anna found, very thankfully, that she could follow his French even though it seemed to be in the local patois.

'I have brought the wife of *monsieur*. She wishes to see her husband and have him released. She knows that he is not a spy.'

'I will go and ask,' said the guard and disappeared into the building.

Pierre took Anna's arm. '*Bon*, it will be easy. He is only a local man. Courage, *ma petite*.'

The guard came back and ushered them into the gendarmerie; a constable greeted them with some reserve.

'You are the wife of M. Peverill?' he asked.

Anna nodded. 'Yes, I am,' she said in French and knew that if she kept to simple words she would be able to maintain a conversation.

'I will ask him if he will see you,' he said, and opened a door behind the official desk.

Anna heard voices with excitement, for she recognized Philippe's lofty tone. I can do it, she told herself, I can do it.

The gendarme reappeared and beckoned to them. 'Come, *madame*, your husband will see you.'

Anna thought that her footsteps faltered, but she reached the doorway. And standing at the other side of the bare room, and not his usual immaculate self, was Philippe. Their eyes met with a deep understanding, he held out his arms to her and without any thought, she ran into them to be gathered close.

'Philippe,' she cried out.

He held her very tightly. '*Ma chérie*, my dear wife, my Anna, you have come to me,' she heard him say. Then she felt his fingers under her chin and again she gazed into his eyes before his lips claimed hers in a long and passionate kiss. She felt herself drowning in the real emotion of the moment, but remembered she had a part to play.

'Philippe, my dear husband, what have they done to you?' she managed to ask in French and throughout, she was able to maintain the conversation in that language so that the two Frenchmen would understand.

'I am all right, my dear one, I waited only for you. Tell me you are well and how are the children?' As he said this, she felt his grip tighten on her arms.

'Christopher is with my mother at Ponderfields,' she told him in a steady voice. 'And little Caroline has stayed with her nurse at Hatherley Park. You are not to worry about them. We will be with them soon, I am sure.'

'*Madame?*' She heard a voice from behind her and looked across the room. The gendarme was staring at her fiercely; Pierre, at his side, was trying to hide a smile of satisfaction.

'Yes, *monsieur*?' she said, as she turned.

'Monsieur is your husband? I can see that it is so, but how did I know he was not the spy for England?'

Anna lifted her head. 'I can assure you that Monsieur Peverill is an English country gentleman and that we live with our children at Hatherley Park in Somerset. It is a big fine estate—'

'But *monsieur* was in France, Madame Peverill.'

'Of course he was in France. As soon as we heard that your Napoleon had abdicated and King Louis XVIII was again in Paris, Philippe set off to see his mother in the capital. He did not tell you? Yes, of course he did. His mother is Madame Poincaré and has been in Paris all these years while the two countries have been at war. It has not been safe for Philippe to travel to see her before. Now he travels, and you stop him. *Que vous êtes bêtise.*'

Anna, almost out of breath with the effort she had made, turned again to Philippe. 'Did you not tell them all this, *mon cher*?'

And she saw the proud Philippe face the gendarme. His voice was icy. 'I hope you are satisfied. It is exactly as I told you and you chose not to believe me. You have held me in this insanitary place all this time. You did not believe me, do you believe my wife? You will realize that I have not spoken a single word to her before this moment, and that she is speaking the truth from her heart. Will you now let me return to my home and my children?'

The gendarme was still looking at Anna and with some respect. 'You speak very good French, Madame Peverill.'

'Of course I do.' She was amused at being addressed thus, but she echoed Philippe's tone. 'We learn French with our governesses in England and I was fortunate to have a mamselle for two years; she taught me all she could. Philippe and I often speak together in French for me to practise when I meet Madame Poincaré one day. Not only that, Christopher knows some French words and so will little Caroline in time, she is only a year old, you know. We wish to get back to the darling so badly, I am sure you will not detain us longer.'

She paused and then spoke more quietly. 'I can see that you are a compassionate man and will probably have a family of your own. You will know what it is like to be separated from your wife and children.' She paused once again, wondering if she had gone far enough; she felt almost exhausted. 'If we can reach Cherbourg today, we can sail to England first thing tomorrow morning and we will be with our loved ones in time before they go to bed. You have the kindness in your eyes, *mon ami*, you will let us go now?'

The gendarme moved forward and stood before them. 'I believe what you have told me, *madame*, and if it is indeed true that our king is in Paris, then I will let you go. Monsieur Peverill, I apologize for my mistake. *Madame*, I wish you a safe journey home and I admire your defence of your husband. I will tell the guard that you are free.'

Minutes later, Pierre was holding the reins, Philippe was helping Anna up into the gig and they drove quickly down the village street. Anna turned to Philippe, buried her face in his shoulder and burst into tears.

'My love,' he murmured, and she wondered if she had imagined the words. 'You are a remarkable girl, Anna; I was not mistaken in you.' He gave a chuckle. 'I think we gave a very convincing performance of a gentleman separated from his wife. I will always remember it. Anna, is my little Carrie all right? She was not too worried at my imprisonment....?' he broke off as he saw her expression. 'What is it?' he asked quietly.

'Do you call Caroline *Carrie?*'

He nodded. 'Yes, I do. It is a shame really for Caroline is a lovely name. But she has always been my little Carrie. Why do you ask?'

'Philippe, when you were in that fever, you kept saying *carry* something and I thought you were meaning that you had a heavy load to carry. I did tell you. But you must have been referring to Caroline, I can see it now.'

'Yes, it was a relief at the time to know that was the main word on my lips, I will explain it all one day. But you found her all right? Did she read my letter? I told Pierre to show it to her. Did you like her? My little girl?'

'Philippe, there has been an upset in Weymouth and I will tell you about it in a moment. But first of all, I must tell you that Caroline came as a tremendous shock to me.'

'Why ever was that, Anna? I don't understand you.' He still had his arm around her and she felt somehow content to stay close to him.

'I thought she was your mistress.'

She felt his arms tighten. 'Goddammit, what ever made you think that... no, you do not need to answer. It was the gossip of the village.'

'And Thora implied it,' Anna told him.

'Thora? She knows better. She must have been trying to make mischief.'

'I think she is jealous. She is afraid I will take you from her.'

'I will have you know, young lady, that I have no intention whatsoever towards Thora. Why should I when I have such a nice little wife already.'

'Fiddle,' came the quick reply from Anna, then she added thoughtfully, 'I think I did quite well.'

'You were most convincing and you have me wishing that you really are my wife. I will have to think about it . . . but, Anna, why did you say that there had been an upset in Weymouth?'

She proceeded to tell him about Tante Michelle and how they had sent Caroline to West Wilton on the stage with Dorcas.

He listened in silence, and then he bent forward and kissed her on the cheek. 'Anna, my dear girl, I am more in your debt than ever. My poor sister, Marie, was always frail; she is probably ill after having yet another child. She has a large brood already, but she loves them all and her husband is very good to her. It was like Michelle to go off immediately though she should have made sure of the good Mrs Belcher before she left Carrie. Are you sure she will have been all right on the stage?'

'Pierre made sure of everything and she will be left at the rectory. I wrote letters to Mrs Boyd and to Mama. And I told Mrs Boyd to let Christopher know.'

'And what is that supposed to mean?'

'As soon as I saw Caroline, I thought of Christopher. I think they are made for each other,' replied Anna. 'You would not object to Caroline being the wife of a respectable country parson? I am going to busy myself with some match-making.'

Philippe held her away from him and met dancing eyes. 'I thought Christopher was relying on you, *ma chère*.'

'And so he is, but I do not love him in that way. He will fall in love with Caroline as soon as he sees her. I am sure of it.'

'You little minx, I think I deserve another kiss.'

'No, you cannot, Philippe, Pierre is with us.'

'Pierre was in the room when you greeted me as my loving wife,' he reminded her.

'That was a pretend kiss,' said a newly pert Anna.

'It did not seem like a pretend kiss to me,' he said.

'I am a good actress, I know it now.'

'Minx,' he said again and, tipping her bonnet away from her face, he found her lips with his and they clung together as much in relief that their ordeal was over, as in any show of affection.

'Thank you, Anna,' he smiled. 'You are indeed a good actress. That was very nice.'

'I am sure I do not know what Pierre will think. But, Philippe. . . .'

'What is it, my love?'

'I am not your love and I do wish you would not keep saying it . . . but, Philippe, you are shivering. What is it?'

'I don't know, I must admit to feeling shivery, but I put it down to being out in the cool fresh air after being shut up in that stuffy room for over a week . . . the only exercise I had was a walk to the privy.'

'Philippe!' Anna sounded shocked but she felt like giggling; this was a Philippe she was yet to know and very far removed from the Mr Peverill of Hatherley Park.

'What is it, my love . . . I am sorry . . . my dear Anna? Surely I cannot shock a young lady who journeyed all the way across the English Channel to pretend to be the wife of a supposed spy.'

'You know you should not mention such things to a lady, even if we are on an absurd cart in the middle of the French countryside. Look, even Pierre is smiling, he is shocked, too.'

Pierre took his eyes off the reins and the horse. 'Miss Anna, if you had been in the employment of *monsieur* for as many years as I have, you would realize that nothing would shock. I think that he said it on purpose to try and shock you. But, *monsieur*, are you indeed shivering? I hope it is not a return of the fever.'

'I hope so, too,' said Mr Philippe Peverill and lapsed into silence.

By the time they reached the outskirts of Cherbourg, it was obvious that Philippe was becoming feverish.

Pierre had to help him down from the cart and M. and Mme. Barnard came to the door.

There was no doubt at their pleasure in seeing him and of their concern for his health, even though Philipppe insisted that it was nothing and that he would be fit to travel on the following day.

They gave him their own bedroom which was next to Anna's and moved into one of the servant's rooms in the attics. Mme. Barnard was solicitous and practical. 'Do not worry, *mademoiselle*,' she said to Anna. 'We have seen him in a fever before, though on the last occasion, he insisted on travelling back to England.'

Anna told the good Frenchwoman what had happened on that occasion and how it was she who had come to nurse him.

'*Bon*,' was the reply. 'We will nurse him between us and Pierre can help. Now I will go to the market to buy lemons – we can get them from the south of the country – so I can make him drink plenty. And we will fetch *le médecin* to him if he gets worse.'

Philippe did get worse and *le médecin* came and ordered a saline draught; Mme. Barnard and Anna took it in turn to sit with him.

In the hours that she listened to his ramblings – this time mainly in French – Anna had many rueful thoughts.

It is almost as though I have brought on the fever by lying to Mama; what started out as pretence has become reality, the only difference being that we are in Cherbourg and not in Weymouth.

And when she heard Philippe repeat Carrie again and again, she now knew that he was thinking of the young daughter he cared for so much. He would also say *Anna* and *femme* and, in spite of her worry, it made her smile. The same words persisted that she had heard on the occasion of his first fever, the words which had puzzled her before, door and salt and something about an evil, but they still made no sense.

Mme. Barnard insisted on Anna taking a walk each day with Pierre to accompany her and she was pleased to find that they were only a few minutes from the harbour.

Cherbourg was both a fishing port and a naval station and it was the fishing port which was nearest the Barnards' house. Anna loved to see the small craft coming back with their catch, the noisy seagulls overhead, the fish-market traders setting up their stalls.

Pierre would laugh at her. 'Miss Anna, it is not really a place for a young lady of fashion.'

'Bah,' she would reply. 'I never was very fashionable and it is all so interesting.'

'But the smell, Miss Anna.'

She looked at him surprised. 'It is only the smell of fish, there is nothing wrong with that. At the end of the day, it is all washed down and the boats are ready to go out again the next morning.'

He looked at her earnest young face. 'It is no wonder that the master thinks so highly of you, for you are not like the young ladies he would meet in the London drawing-rooms.'

'I cannot imagine Philippe in a London drawing-room,' she said thoughtfully.

'It is a long time ago, Miss Anna, I think he is changed now and I am not permitted to say more.'

'Do you worry when he has these fevers, Pierre? Has he had them before?'

'Yes, they started in Spain, but always he makes the recover, as you say. But it alarms me what he says when he is delirious,' he said somewhat soberly.

'A lot of it is nonsense, Pierre. He calls your name and it is always Carrie ... Carrie, I know now what he means. Do you think she will worry that we have not returned?'

He shook his head. '*Non*, not that one. She is used to his coming and going; she cannot remember anything else and always she has Tante Michelle. This time she has your dear mother, so she will be well cared for. Do not worry, Miss Anna.'

'I wonder if we should have sent a letter to her; at least we could tell her that he is out of the gaol and safely back in Cherbourg.'

'I think not, *mademoiselle*, we would have to tell her about the fever and that would not do. And also we must keep Captain Hart standing by with the *Marie-Rose*. In a few days, M. Philippe will be well enough to travel to Weymouth and the cutter must be there ready for him.'

'You think of everything, Pierre.'

'I have to, Miss Anna, it is my duty.'

'I am not really worried about Caroline; she will like it at Ponderfields and I am hoping that a great friend of mine will visit her and perhaps take her riding, or to look round Bath.'

And she told Pierre about Christopher and his grin told her that she had pleased him.

EIGHT

IF ANNA AND Pierre had had second sight, they would have seen a very happy and interested Caroline travelling through Dorset and then into Somerset. The stage stopped at Ilchester just as Anna had done on her journey with Pierre in the opposite direction.

Dorcas was equally happy with the journey in the stagecoach and the two of them chatted continually to themselves to the amusement of their fellow passengers, who consisted of a fat farm woman and three elderly gentleman.

Caroline did not feel in a worry about her father because she felt confident that Pierre and Anna would bring him safely home. What pleased her more than anything was that she was at last going to see the Hatherley Park she had heard so much about. She had met Thora in Weymouth before the move to Hatherley was made and had not taken to her, for she thought that Thora had assumed a proprietorial air over the gentleman who was introduced as her cousin. Caroline was resigned to the fact that one day her father would marry again, but she hoped it would not be to Thora. Now that she had met Anna, she knew well where her hopes lay.

The stagecoach pulled up outside the rectory in West Wilton at exactly three o'clock, the coachman helped them down and took their luggage to the front door. Dorcas and Caroline followed and Caroline could not stop the feeling of apprehension which came over her.

Then the door was opened and a bewildered but kindly Mrs Boyd stood there, looking puzzled.

'The stagecoach stopping at the rectory, whatever next and who...?' She stopped speaking and gazed from Caroline to Dorcas and back again.

Caroline knew that she should speak first, but it was not easy. 'Are you Mrs Boyd?' she asked tentatively. 'I am sorry to trouble you, I am Caroline Peverill. I have a letter for you from Miss Anna Starkie whom I believe to be a near neighbour of yours.'

Mrs Boyd stared. 'You are a Peverill? And Anna gone to Weymouth because poor Mr Peverill has a return of the fever? You had better come in. I will offer you some refreshment and then you can explain it all to me, for I am sure that I cannot understand anything.'

In the drawing-room, Mrs Boyd ordered tea to be brought in and took the letter which Caroline was holding out to her. Caroline saw her frown as she read it, and then give a smile. 'You are Mr Peverill's daughter and his family is in Weymouth? We had no idea that he had a daughter. We thought that—' Mrs Boyd stopped in horror and put a hand to her mouth. 'Oh, I am very sorry...'

But Caroline was laughing and Mrs Boyd was more confused than ever.

'I understand, Mrs Boyd, do not worry. Anna said just the same when she arrived at our Weymouth house; she thought I was Mr Peverill's mistress. Is it not shocking? But I think a rumour was spread around West Wilton and Papa did nothing to stop it.

Indeed, I do believe that it amused him to let people believe it.'

'Miss Peverill—' Mrs Boyd started to say.

'No, please call me Caroline and let me explain everything to you. This is Dorcas, she has been my maid since I was born and I will not be parted from her, so please let her stay in the drawing-room with me. My mama died when I was born and I have been brought up by Papa's sister, I call her Tante Michelle. All the Peverills are partly French and have French names. Papa has the fever again and Anna was so good to come to him; he kept calling for her, you know. Anna was afraid that I would catch the fever so she sent me on the stagecoach to her mama, and of course, it was all quite proper travelling on the stage as I had Dorcas with me. To be truthful, we both enjoyed the journey immensely. Now if you would be good enough, could you direct us to Anna's mama? I also have a letter for Mrs Starkie, and Anna assures me that her mother will be delighted to have me stay with her.'

Mrs Boyd was, by now, all smiles; she had read the *post scriptum* to her note and knew exactly what Anna meant by it. She had always known, in her heart of hearts, that Christopher and Anna would never make a match of it.

'I will ask Jeremy – he is the eldest son I have at home – to take you in the gig. It is of no inconvenience at all, Ponderfields is less than a mile distant but away from the road; that is why dear Anna asked for you to be set down here. And I am very glad she did for it has been delightful to meet you and to know that Mr Peverill has such a lovely daughter. No, I do not put you to the blush for I mean it very sincerely.'

Caroline could see that Mrs Boyd was still holding Anna's letter and could not stop her next question. 'Mrs Boyd, Anna let me read the note. Will you tell me who Christopher is?'

Mrs Boyd smiled. 'She is a wicked girl! Christopher is my second eldest son – John, our eldest boy, has been in the Peninsula, you know, and there has been such good news from Lord Wellington that we hope to have John home again soon – but I am sorry, my dear, I am wandering. Christopher has been at Oxford reading for the church and he has just got his preferment. He is now the Vicar of Battiscombe, only six miles from here. Christopher has always had hopes of Anna becoming his wife, but the naughty girl keeps refusing him. However, I am sure that she loves him dearly for they have been brought up together with the two houses being so close. I am sure that Christopher will be visiting us very soon and that you will meet him.'

'I would like to meet any friend of Anna's,' Caroline replied politely.

Mrs Boyd got up and walked to the door. 'Now you and Dorcas just sit there for a few minutes and I will go and ask Jeremy to bring the gig round to the front door.'

Caroline was not to know that as soon as they had left the rectory, Mrs Boyd sent one of the servants to Battiscombe with a message asking Christopher to come as soon as possible.

It seemed no more than minutes before they were travelling in the gig up the drive to Ponderfields and Caroline was bracing herself for her introduction to Anna's mother. She had taken Anna's letter out of her reticule and was holding it tightly in her hand.

Jeremy had received instructions from his mother to go in and find Mrs Starkie and explain the situation to her very briefly.

And so it was that Caroline and Dorcas were greeted with open arms.

'I cannot believe it,' said Mrs Starkie as she took them into the drawing-room. 'Caroline Peverill, and to think that all the time, Mr Peverill had a daughter and did not tell us. I am very pleased to have you here, Caroline. Dorcas, would you go and find Betsy – she is probably in the kitchen with Cook – and ask her to put

Caroline in the guest-room and tell her you are to have the little room next to it, for it was always meant for a lady's maid.' She turned to Caroline. 'My dear, you have me all of a twitter; now, I must read the letter which Anna has written to me. I do hope that your papa is not as poorly as he was last time. Anna was over at Hatherley Park for more than a week.' She paused to sit opposite Caroline and to read the letter making comments as she went along.

'And you with no mama, Caroline,' she said.

'Oh, but I have my Tante Michelle,' replied Caroline.

'I believe that I am right in thinking that Mr Peverill's mother was French,' observed Mrs Starkie.

'Yes, she is still living in France. I think that Papa hopes to go and see her now that Lord Wellington is on the way to Paris.'

'But Anna has done the right thing in sending you to me, Caroline. She is a sensible girl and she did not want you exposed to the fever. It will be a relief to your dear papa, as well. And to think we had no idea that Mr Peverill had a family in Weymouth; it just proves that we should never listen to gossip.'

Caroline smiled to herself, but dared not again make mention of her papa's supposed mistress in Weymouth. 'It is very kind of you to have me at such short notice, Mrs Starkie.'

'It is the greatest of pleasure, for I miss Anna so much. She is more than a daughter to me since the loss of Mr Starkie; she is my friend and companion. Has she told you that we have three younger girls still in the schoolroom?'

'Yes, she said their names were Felicity, Selina and Jane; perhaps we will all be able to walk out together. I long to walk in the countryside. I like Weymouth very much, but we live near the harbour so there are only the walks along the promenade. Weymouth is quite fashionable, you know.'

'Yes, I do believe it is since dear, poor King George made it popular. It seems that the Prince of Wales prefers to be in Brighton.'

Caroline nodded. 'Yes, it is all the rage to be in Brighton. And, Mrs Starkie, I would like to see Hatherley Park very much. I have heard so much about it from Papa.'

'And you know Miss Peverill? She will be your cousin, too.'

'I think she is about my third cousin if there is such a thing,' Caroline laughed. 'It is quite a distant relationship. I have met her and she is a Peverill after all, so I must respect her.'

Mrs Starkie looked at the young girl closely. 'You sound as though you hold her in dislike.'

'No, it is not quite as bad as that. She is a very well-meaning person, but she is older than Papa and I had the feeling when I met her that she was trying to win his affection.'

'You are certainly right, my dear, for she has let it be known that she hopes to be the next Mrs Peverill.'

'Yes, I can quite imagine it,' replied Caroline, and preferred to change the subject. 'Mrs Boyd has been telling me of her son, Christopher. Is it true that he wishes to marry Anna?'

'Oh yes, Caroline, such a romance. They have been attached to each other for many years, but Anna keeps him waiting for his reply. Now he has the parish of Battiscombe with a fine vicarage and it is my hope – and my wish – that they will settle down there together.'

'I would like to meet him,' said Caroline.

'He will be here as soon as Anna returns,' said Anna's mother. 'You will meet him then.'

In fact, Caroline was destined to meet Christopher much sooner than that.

On her first day at Ponderfields, Mrs Starkie went with Caroline in the carriage to visit Miss Peverill at Hatherley Park. She ordered George-Coachman to drive slowly through the grounds so that Caroline could look around her.

'It is so lovely,' Caroline kept saying. 'The parkland and the trees... oh, and now we can see the house. It is much larger than I had imagined. I do not wonder at Thora wanting to be its mistress, but I think Papa will have something to say in the matter.'

Hatherley was indeed a splendid house; it was built at the time of the first King George and in the biscuit-coloured Bath stone, now deepened and mellowed with age. It was very formal in design but had a dignified symmetry typical of the country houses of the time.

Soon they were driving through the formal gardens at the front of the house and Caroline was rapt in her admiration. 'Mrs Starkie, it is a beautiful place. I wonder at Papa leaving it so often to come to us in Weymouth.'

'But, Caroline my dear,' Mrs Starkie was not one to be reticent if she was curious about a certain thing, 'why is it that you and your aunt are still in the Weymouth house when you could be living in such style here at Hatherley Park?'

There was a long pause before Caroline spoke and Mrs Starkie wondered if the young girl had been upset at not moving into Somerset.

'Papa said, you see Mrs Starkie, that although he thought I would like it here at Hatherley and that it was a lovely house, it had been very much neglected and he wanted to have it renovated before he brought me here. Thora was going to keep house for him and she said that she did not mind enduring the noise and discomfort of the builders and workmen around her.'

'But there has been no sign of any renovation,' said Mrs Starkie instantly.

'Has there not? Perhaps Papa was waiting until he was beforehand with the world before he got the builders in. Ah, here we are.' Caroline seemed glad of an interruption to the somewhat awkward conversation for, as she had told Anna earlier, she had never been told the reason for the move to Hatherley Park; she had had to invent an excuse for not coming to Hatherley to satisfy Mrs Starkie and had felt herself floundering.

They were shown in and a flustered Thora came rushing from the back of the house. 'Mrs Starkie, how very nice to see you. I am afraid you catch me at a disadvantage, but ... Caroline, what in God's name are *you* doing here?'

Mrs Starkie stared. Miss Peverill had spoken quite vulgarly in her surprise at seeing Caroline; she was generally considered to be a most superior lady, as well as being a cousin of Mr Peverill. But Caroline was making her reply and Mrs Starkie listened carefully.

'Thora, Papa has the fever again. He kept calling for Anna – he did so last time apparently – and Pierre came to fetch her to Weymouth. She is very kind. Not only that, she insisted that I came to stay with her mama so that I would not be in danger of succumbing to the fever myself. So here I am and Mrs Starkie has been very kind to me. The first thing I wanted to do, of course, was to come and see Hatherley Park for it will be my home one day. As soon as you have finished with the builders, of course, Thora.'

'Yes, Caroline, I am afraid that dear Philippe will be very disappointed that they have not even made a start yet. Now, do come into the drawing-room and I will order some wine. Mrs Starkie, it is very kind of you to have Caroline. It is not generally known that Philippe is a widower and has a daughter living in Weymouth. He is often there himself, of course, but I am very sorry to hear of him having another attack of the fever. It was quite nasty on the last occasion and Anna was so good. She and Mrs Shapter did all the nursing, for I am ashamed to say that I am of very little use in the sick-room. But Anna and your Tante Michelle will look after him,

Caroline, and I am sure we will soon have him with us at Hatherley once again. I had thought Anna to be visiting in Bath, but the dear girl must have said that to save me the worry of Philippe's illness.'

Mrs Starkie thought all this much more in Miss Peverill's usual style and they all chatted over a glass of wine.

Then Caroline had to be shown over the house, and as Mrs Starkie had gone no further than the drawing-room on previous visits, she was included in the tour of inspection. To her eyes, it was far from being shabby and it would seem that very little alteration was needed unless Mr Peverill had ambitious schemes for adding a conservatory at the back of the house. She felt puzzled and even more so when she had reached the foot of the stairs and was standing in the vestibule waiting for Caroline and Miss Peverill.

They were still on the upstairs landing and her sharp ears caught the last words of a whispered argument between the two of them.

'Where is Philippe?' Thora's voice was the loudest but Caroline's light tone was clear when she replied.

'He has the fever in Weymouth, Thora, I told you so.'

Thora's reply came quickly and fiercely, even with a hint of malice. 'I do not believe you. He would never have allowed you to travel on the stage by yourself.'

'I had Dorcas with me.'

'That is not my point, you know that very well, for he could easily have sent you in the carriage with Pierre. It is my belief that he is still in France—'

'Hush, Thora, we must not speak of it. Mrs Starkie will hear us.'

Mrs Starkie had heard every word and went back to Ponderfields sensing that things were not as they seemed. First of all, Mr Peverill makes no mention of having a daughter or any family in Weymouth, then Anna is called away hurriedly because he is ill, soon after that, Caroline appears on her own at Ponderfields and now here is Miss Peverill talking about her cousin being in France. I will ask Anna when she returns and I will have to hope that she has not got herself involved in this apparent mystery.

Next day, all her doubts and musings over the Peverill family were forgotten with the arrival on the scene of the Rev Christopher Boyd.

He walked into the rectory and went in search of his mother. She was pleased to see him.

'Christopher, you have come straight away, that is good of you.'

'I thought perhaps that you or Father were unwell,' he replied, having greeted her with an affectionate kiss on the cheek.

'No, we are both keeping well. It is just that something unexpected has happened and I thought that if you could spare a few days from your duties, you might be able to help us.'

'You sound very mysterious, Mama.'

She gave a laugh and told him of her suspicions.

He laughed then. 'You have a vivid imagination, Mama. I cannot conceive of a more respectable gentleman than Mr Philippe Peverill and you know that I would never listen to those tales which went around the village. So why have I been called in to help?'

'Can you stay a little while, Christopher? Will your curate take care of things for you?'

When Christopher had procured the living of Battiscombe, he had inherited an elderly curate who had been there for some years and did not have either the qualifications or the qualities – or indeed, the wish – to become vicar. He knew everyone in the village and had immediately treated Christopher as though he was a favourite son and not his superior.

'Joshua is used to running the parish,' Christopher told his mother. 'They were six months without a vicar before I was appointed. He is not young, but he is a good man as long as he is allowed to go about things at his own slow pace; he is much loved in Battiscombe. But you have not answered my question, Mama. What can I do to help in this little mystery of yours?'

'It is Caroline,' she told him.

'And who is Caroline?'

Mrs Boyd stared at her son bemused for a moment. 'Oh my goodness me, you have no idea who Caroline is, have you? It has all happened in these last few days.'

'Am I allowed to know what has happened, Mama?' he asked her, with some amusement and a hint of curiosity.

'Come and sit down and we will have some coffee and I will tell you the whole story. It is quite intriguing.'

And they sipped their coffee and Mrs Boyd told Christopher about Mr Peverill's illness, Anna's disappearance and Caroline's arrival.

'She is such a nice girl but she has no one here of her own age, though, of course, Mrs Starkie will be very kind to her. There are the younger girls, but they are still in the schoolroom, as you know. I thought perhaps you could go riding with her, or maybe take her for walks.'

Christopher looked at his mother suspiciously. 'Mama, you are not trying to match-make are you, by any chance?'

Mrs Boyd succeeded in looking horrified. 'Christopher, how can you suggest such a thing when I know how devoted you are to Anna? It would be a kindness and Anna is sure to be pleased that Caroline is not all on her own while she is staying here.'

'Mama, I have to believe you. I will ride over to Ponderfields immediately. Is she a pretty girl?'

'You will see, Christopher.'

At Ponderfields, Mrs Starkie greeted him with some surprise.

'Christopher, how very nice to see you. Did you know that I have a young lady visitor?'

'Yes, Mama told me. In fact, she sent for me.' He knew that this information would intrigue her.

'Sent for you? Goodness gracious, whatever is she thinking of?'

'She thought it would please Anna that Miss Peverill had company of her own age,' he told her, and waited for her reply.

'She is quite right, but I do hope you will not go falling in love with Caroline, or Anna will be very put out.'

He smiled. 'I have a feeling that Anna would be very pleased; she still refuses me, you know.'

'Yes, I know, the naughty girl. Now, it so happens that Caroline has gone walking with Miss Swinburne and the girls. I think that they have gone in the direction of Hatherley. Will you wait or would you like to go and meet them?'

'I think I will walk out and meet them, Mrs Starkie.' Christopher started across the fields towards Hatherley with a feeling of curiosity about the visitor to Ponderfields; his mother had not called him from Battiscombe for the reason she had given, of that he was certain.

He heard the sound of girlish chatter before he saw the group emerging from Hatherley Wood. He was puzzled. There was no doubt that it was the tall Miss Swinburne, but it seemed that she had four schoolroom misses with her.

He stood still and watched, but was soon spotted by Selina and three of the party shrieked his name and started running towards him.

'Christopher,' came the cries, as they flung himself into his arms in a manner which would earn Miss Swinburne's disapproval when she reached them.

But Christopher did not hear their cries and scarcely gave them a greeting in spite of him being a favourite of theirs.

He was staring at the remaining small figure now coming up to them, wearing a pelisse of bright blue and a bonnet of a paler blue from which escaped dark curls. There was a half-smile in the blue eyes of the prettiest girl he had ever seen. Then their eyes met and Christopher Boyd was lost.

While Miss Swinburne scolded her charges for their boisterous and unladylike behaviour, Caroline found herself being held captive by the gaze of the tall young man she had heard the girls call Christopher, who appeared to be a gentleman of the cloth.

Then she heard Miss Swinburne's voice. 'Oh, Miss Caroline, I do apologize for the girls' behaviour, they have known Mr Christopher all their lives. Please let me introduce you. This is Mr Christopher – oh, I am sorry, I am forgetting myself – the Reverend Christopher Boyd, he is the Boyds' second son and has recently become the vicar of Battiscombe. Mr Christopher, this is Miss Caroline Peverill, only daughter of Mr Peverill of Hatherley Park. Perhaps you would like to talk to each other while I keep the girls from being too unruly.'

Caroline found her hand in the strong grasp of the young man.

'I am very pleased to meet you, Miss Peverill; in fact, I have to confess to coming to search for you when I did not find you at Ponderfields. Mrs Starkie told me that you were out walking with Miss Swinburne.'

Caroline was glad of the time these simple words afforded her. For her mind was working furiously as she remembered the *Post scriptum* in Anna's letter to Mrs Boyd. *I think Caroline might do for Christopher*, Anna had said. Did she now know the meaning of the cryptic message? How was she to behave if this was the Christopher in question?

Caroline had been brought up to be polite and her upbringing did not fail her now. 'Mr Boyd, I am very pleased to meet you. Your mother very kindly received me at the rectory and your brother, Jeremy, drove me to Ponderfields.'

'Shall we walk along?' he asked her. 'Perhaps I might call you Caroline? And please call me Christopher, as Anna does.'

Caroline just came up to his shoulder and she liked the protective feeling of his height alongside her. She had a quivering sensation which she must hide immediately because she knew that Christopher was pledged to Anna. And yet Anna had used those words at the end of her letter. Why, she kept asking herself, why?

At the same time, Christopher was experiencing an alarming desire to take Caroline in his arms and to love and protect her for the rest of his life. How can one possibly be overcome with such feelings in just a few minutes? he was asking himself. And how is it that I have never felt like this when I have been with Anna?

'Caroline, would you like to come riding with me tomorrow morning?' He thought speech and action to be the safest way in his startling predicament. 'I am here at home for a few days.'

They were walking slowly and Caroline looked up at him. 'It is very kind of you to ask me, but I am afraid that I do not ride.'

He stopped, so Caroline did the same and they stood facing one another.

Christopher's words were almost disbelieving. 'You do not ride?' he asked.

Caroline had to smile at his astonishment. 'No, I have never ridden. You see, first of all we lived in London and it was considered an expense to keep stables; we could always get a chair or a hackney carriage when we wanted to go out, and Papa walked everywhere when he was at home. He was in the Foreign Office, you know. Then we moved to Weymouth and it seemed to be more the thing to stroll along the promenade when we wanted exercise, though Papa does keep a carriage. I have surprised you?'

He nodded as they took up their walk again. 'Yes, you see, growing up here in Somerset, we have all learned to ride. Anna and I have ridden together since she had her first pony.' He paused.

'Did you like Anna? It was very caring of her to go to your papa, but then she was very good to go to Hatherley when Mr Peverill was ill the first time. I am sorry to hear that he has a fever again. But, Caroline, I do not understand why you had to come on the stage when Mr Peverill has a carriage.'

Caroline gave an inward groan as she realized that she was going to have to tell yet more lies; true that the carriage was safely in Weymouth, but there was no Pierre to drive it. 'Everything seemed to happen at once,' she told him, trying to sound convincing. 'Papa was ill, Anna arrived, and we had a message to say that my Tante Marie in London was also ill; so Tante Michelle went off to London in the carriage, and it was then that Anna decided that I should come here. The only thing for Dorcas and myself was to travel on the stage It was quite a novel experience.'

Christopher said thoughtfully, 'But it does mean that it has brought you here.'

Caroline was regaining her confidence. 'And is that supposed to mean anything?' she asked, quite pertly.

He smiled down at her. 'Yes, I think it does. Even if we cannot ride together, we could perhaps walk in the mornings, if it is fine. We could stroll in Hatherley Wood. Your papa is away so there will be no shooting taking place and it is the close season in any case. Would you like to do that?'

They were almost at the house and found Mrs Starkie standing on the porch steps with the children. 'I am so pleased that the two of you have met,' she said. 'It will be company for Caroline, so do not stand on ceremony, Christopher. Come whenever you like as you did when Anna was here.

'Thank you, Mrs Starkie.' He turned to Caroline. 'We will walk in the wood in the morning then, Caroline, and you will be most welcome to come back to the rectory for luncheon. Mama will be pleased to see you again.'

Caroline watched him go and turned to Mrs Starkie. 'He is a very pleasant young gentleman,' she remarked. She was longing to go to her room so that she could calm her disordered feelings.

'One could not ask for better as a son-in-law,' said Mrs Starkie happily. 'I do declare that Anna refuses him as a tease. There has never been anyone else for Anna and I am certain of a successful outcome.'

'I do hope so,' replied Caroline, with some misgiving. 'I will just take my pelisse and bonnet up to my room, Mrs Starkie.'

In her room, Caroline sat herself on the window seat staring at the garden at the front of the house; beyond that the fields and the wood where she had walked that morning. She imagined that she could see the exact place where she had met Christopher Boyd.

She did not realize that her thoughts on their meeting were almost identical to those of Christopher. However can I have these turbulent feelings on meeting a young gentleman for the first time? It is almost as though I have fallen in love, yet it must be impossible to love someone whom you have known for only ten minutes. I will put all these thoughts behind me for I must think of Anna. However, I think I can trust myself to behave with some propriety and I will allow myself to look forward to the walk in the wood tomorrow.

NINE

CAROLINE WAITED EAGERLY for Christopher's arrival the next morning, although there had been rain before breakfast and she was afraid that it was going to be a day of April showers.

Christopher, however, was in cheerful mood and brushed her fears aside. 'We can always shelter in the wood if it comes on to rain. I trust that you have sensible shoes for walking across the fields.'

She grinned. 'I will not shame you by venturing into the countryside in my pumps; I brought my half-boots hoping to be able to enjoy a country walk. But it is kind of you to consider me.'

This augured a successful outing, but within ten minutes they were involved in a spat with each other, which could not quite be called a quarrel.

'How long can you be absent from Battiscombe?' Caroline asked. They were walking slowly over the fields towards the wood.

'I think I will wait until Anna returns so that you are not on your own,' he replied easily.

'I expect you look forward to seeing her.'

'Yes, no doubt.'

Caroline glanced up at him. His reply had not been enthusiastic and she was unable to gauge his mood. She did not know him well enough, and found herself with a forbidden yearning of wanting to know him better.

'Why do you sound so hesitant?' she asked him.

He stopped and for long moments stood looking down at her. 'A certain young lady has come between me and my wish to see Anna.'

She knew his meaning and rebuked him sharply. 'Balderdash, you have not known me for twenty-four hours yet, for I am sure that you are talking about me. And if you think that I will come between you and Anna, then I will turn round and go straight back to Ponderfields.' Even as she spoke, Caroline felt the first drops of rain on her face.

'You will do no such thing for we are in for another of those heavy showers. We had better hurry into the wood until it passes over.'

The wood was some thirty yards away and Christopher took Caroline's hand and they started to run towards the trees. Before they reached the wood, they were both very wet, out of breath and laughing.

Under the shelter of a large oak, Christopher kept hold of her hand and drew her towards him. She rested her head unthinkingly against his chest while she tried to regain her breath; she was panting and unable to speak, let alone protest because he had pulled her into his arms.

'Caroline.' His voice sounded strange and she glanced up, immediately startled by the expression in his eyes. 'I want to kiss you.'

Caroline regained control of herself very quickly, pulled herself away from him and started to run from under the trees back into the open field. Christopher was quickly at her side and caught up with her before she was once again in the heavy rain.

'Caroline, I am sorry. I should not have said it. Something has happened to me since I met you and the wild Christopher of my youth has replaced the sober vicar of Battiscombe. Please forgive me, but you must know that you are captivating.'

'I am nothing of the kind,' she snapped back at him. 'I am small and I am ordinary, and not only that, you are betrothed to Anna.'

'I am not betrothed to Anna; every time I ask her to be my wife, she refuses me,' he countered.

'She will give in to you one day, she must do,' Caroline replied sturdily, but all the time remembering the words on Anna's note. *I think Caroline might do for Christopher.* However, she went on speaking to Christopher as though she had not been reminded of the message. 'Not only that, Mrs Starkie thinks that you will make a splendid son-in-law, she told me so.'

He smiled ruefully. 'I think that my mother and Mrs Starkie planned it together when we were born! I promise you that I won't let Anna down; it is not in my nature to go back on an arrangement such as that.' They stood together under the oak staring at the falling rain. 'Now that I have met you, I will be the strictest and most proper young gentleman you have ever known if you will allow me to take you about until Anna comes home. What do you say, Caroline?'

She looked up at him. She liked him, she liked him more than she dared to think; she had a shaky feeling that she would have enjoyed it if he had kissed her. 'Thank you, Christopher,' she succeeded in saying. 'I will trust in good friendship and I would be very pleased to have your company for a few days.'

'And now the rain is stopping, so I think we will go straight back to the house and get you into dry clothes. I have the dog-cart at Ponderfields so when you have changed, I will take you over to the rectory where Mama will have a luncheon ready for us. I would like you to meet my father. You have already met Jeremy; young

Matthew is still in the schoolroom, he takes lessons with Papa. You know, it has always been rather a jest between the two families that one should have four girls and the other four boys. I think that both mamas would have matched them all if they could have done.'

Caroline was so pleased to return to such pleasant topics after the emotional moments in the wood, that she hurried over the wet grass at Christopher's side relishing the idea of a few days spent in his company.

In the end, she felt that the next few days passed all too quickly; there was no news from Weymouth, but she tried not to worry, hoping with all her heart that Pierre and Anna had secured her father's release from his French captors.

She felt warm with comfort at Christopher's kind intentions. He had come from Battiscombe in his gig and he insisted on showing her the area of his birth and his upbringing.

They went on a day trip into Bath where they had luncheon at the York House Hotel and they toured the Abbey, the Roman Baths and, last of all, the Pump Room where Caroline made a face when Christopher coaxed her into trying a glass of the famous healing water.

On the Sunday, they all attended service at the church in West Wilton; the Rev Boyd took the service, but Christopher had been persuaded to preach the sermon. He took as his text. *To everything there is a season, and a time to every purpose under the heaven: . . . a time to weep and a time to laugh . . . a time to keep silence and a time to speak . . .*' from the third chapter of Ecclesiastes.

Caroline found herself mesmerized by him; his light-hearted words followed by seriousness, his kindly words for the congregation, his admonition at their failings and the neglect of their duties. He spoke to them all, not for a very long time as many did in country parishes, but he seemed to have a message for young and old alike.

She found that the words '*a time to keep silence, a time to speak*' seemed to be aimed directly at her, though there was no way in which Christopher could have known her ambivalent position.

At dinner at the rectory, where all the Boyds and the Starkies were gathered, Mr Boyd had an obvious pride in his son and a kindliness towards his young guest. Caroline ended the day almost sorrowfully as she realized that all this simple rural happiness was not to be for her.

Christopher had only a few days left and still there was no word from Weymouth, so when he suggested a trip to Battiscombe, she agreed with delight. She did not wish to go to Hatherley again and she hoped that a visit to Battiscombe would take her mind off her worried thoughts of her father, Anna and Pierre. Surely they could not all be imprisoned in France? She knew something had gone wrong.

The lanes to Battiscombe were poor, but it was at least dry and they did not have to splash through large puddles in the gig. It was a warm day and Caroline had dispensed with her pelisse and was dressed in a soft blue dress of sprig muslin, carrying a Norwich shawl around her arms.

Christopher said little as they drove along; she thought that he must have something on his mind and wondered if it was because he was taking her, and not Anna, to his new home.

She found Battiscombe to be a large village which lay on the side of a hill in rolling countryside on the border with Wiltshire; the church lay at the end of the village, at its highest point.

Christopher helped her down and she stood still, not looking at the church but at the lovely view across northern Somerset and towards Bath. She could almost imagine that she could pick out West Wilton.

'It *is* a lovely view, is it not?' said Christopher standing at her side. 'I have the same view from some of the windows of the vicarage.

THE PROUD MR PEVERILL

'Is the vicarage down in the village?' Caroline asked, glancing around her and seeing only a handsome stone built house which looked much too imposing to be a vicarage.

'No, that is the vicarge, next to the church. It is very convenient.'

Caroline was both astonished and puzzled. 'But Christopher, it is a very old house and the church looks quite new.'

He nodded. 'Yes, you are quite right, my dear. The vicarage was built almost two hundred years ago; it is a beautiful old building. The church dated back to the twelfth century, but about fifty years ago, there was a fire and most of the church was destroyed beyond repair. So it was rebuilt in the same style and the stones were brought from the Bath quarries. Let me show you round.'

Inside, the church had retained some of its ancient pillars, but all the woodwork was new and shining, the pulpit had beautiful carvings.

'You like it here, Christopher?'

'Yes, I am very fortunate in both church and congregation. Wait till you see the vicarage,' he replied readily.

Caroline was enchanted with the old house. Christopher called to the kitchen for Mrs Farleigh, his cook and housekeeper.

She came hurrying towards them, a small plump woman with a ready smile. 'Well, sir, I didn't think as you was going to return from West Wilton just yet, I must say . . .'

'Mrs Farleigh, I would like you to meet Miss Caroline Peverill of Hatherley Park which is in West Wilton. I have been taking Miss Peverill around the district while her father is away from home. They have recently moved into Hatherley. We have driven over just for the day as I wished her to see Battiscombe.'

Mrs Farleigh bobbed a curtsy. 'You'm the first visitor we've 'ad, miss, and very honoured I am to meet you.' She turned to Christopher. 'And shall I prepare a luncheon for you, sir?'

'Yes, please, Mrs Farleigh. I am going to show Miss Peverill round the house now and then maybe the garden before we return to West Wilton.'

To say that Caroline was enchanted was an understatement. It was indeed a beautiful old house and all she could find to say was 'Oh, Christopher.'

The dining-room in particular drew her ecstasies. 'The panelling,' she breathed, for the whole room was oak panelled and beautifully carved.

Christopher smiled. 'Wait until you see the library, I use it as my study.'

In the library, Caroline looked at the glass-fronted bookcases with awe. 'All the books,' she said. 'Are they all religious volumes?'

Christopher smiled. 'It is not the books I brought you to see. Look up at the ceiling.'

She looked up and gasped. 'It is panelled in plasterwork and what an intricate pattern. Christopher, I have only ever seen ceilings like this in grand houses.' She looked at him curiously. 'Do you like it or would you have preferred something plainer?'

'I do like it, Caroline, and I feel very honoured to live in such a beautiful house. Some vicarages are very plain but my patron is Lord Freshford and the benefice has been in the gift of his family for generations. Their own house is equally beautiful, but much larger, of course. I went there for my interview. Come and see the staircase and I will show you the view from the guest room.'

The broad staircase went up in three short flights, each turning on a short landing, but it was the carved newel posts which Christopher wished her to see.

'I do not think that I have seen a staircase like that before, Christopher, I feel lost for words . . . oh, and I see what you mean by the view. It is all perfect.'

'It lacks only a mistress,' he said, as they went down the stairs into the living-room which had once been the great hall.

There was something in his voice which made Caroline turn sharply and look at him. They were standing in the stone mullioned bay window, overlooking the garden.

'But you are going to marry Anna. She will love it here and I am sure it will be very soon.'

'She has refused me.'

Caroline felt a tautness in the atmosphere and she moved across the room to sit on a wooden settle. 'Christopher, I believe she has been roasting you. She is very fond of you, I am sure of that.'

'I do not believe that fondness is enough.'

Again the tense words and Caroline did not know what to say next. She did not have to find words for Christopher had crossed the room and sat himself close to her on the settle.

'Caroline, I brought you here especially,' he said urgently.

'Especially for what? I thought it was to show me your church and vicarage.' Then she found her hand held tightly in both of his.

'I have brought you here because I want to ask you to marry me. I know that I should ask your father first, but he is not here and he is ill. Caroline, all this week we have been together, I have fallen more deeply in love with you every day. Will you marry me and come as the wife of the vicar of Battiscombe and live in this beautiful old house? Please say that you will.'

Caroline snatched her hand away and sat up very stiffly. Her feelings were tumultuous for she knew, deeply and sincerely, that she loved Christopher Boyd and would like nothing better in life than to be his wife. But it was forbidden to her.

So when she did at last speak, it was very formally. 'Christopher, I have enjoyed our days together, but nothing will make me displace Anna in your affections. She was meant to marry you and she will marry you. Please do not mention the matter again, for by doing so you will spoil a visit which I have enjoyed very much.'

'And what about love?' he asked her.

'What about love? It was you who mentioned it, not me.'

'Caroline, stop playing the statue and look at me and tell me that you do not love me.'

His hands were on her shoulders and she had no choice but to look up at him, her gaze faltered under his.

'Christopher...' she whispered.

'I am going to steal a kiss.'

'No, no...'

But it was no use protesting. His lips on hers were not rough, but gently encouraging, seeking a way to draw from her the words he wanted to hear. For both of them, it was their first kiss and they drew apart and looked at each other with love in their eyes.

Then Caroline remembered Anna and she broke down, her face hidden in her hands.

'No... no... Anna,' were the only words Christopher could make out.

'Caroline I love you, you must know it by now.'

'No, you cannot I will not deal Anna such a turn. How can I? She has gone to save Papa and I do not know what has happened to her; she might be ill, or locked up in prison, or anything. How can I even think of love when everything has gone wrong. Oh, Christopher.'

And she threw herself against him and he held her close as he had done in the wood on that first day together.

'Caroline, whatever is it? You are not making any sense. What is it that you are saying about Anna? Where is she? Have you had no news from her?'

'Nothing, not a letter, or a message, not a single word.'

Christopher guessed that something unknown to him and

worrying to Caroline had occurred and he put all thoughts of love away from him.

'I think you had better tell me, Caroline. I do not need to say that it will be in the strictest confidence. It is something serious, is it not?'

Caroline let herself rest her head against him, glad of his comfort. She drew a deep breath to steady herself and then the words came tumbling out as she told the story, glad to share her burden of worry and guilt with him.

'You are the only person I would tell, Christopher. You will be shocked because we have been living a life of lies.' She looked at him fearfully, half-afraid of his disbelief and anger.

But all he said, and it was said very calmly, was, 'Tell me all, Caroline, and right from the beginning if you can.'

'We moved to Weymouth – that is Papa and Tante Michelle and myself – in 1809. It was before the battle of Talavera and Lord Wellington was still Sir Arthur Wellesley. Papa was in the Foreign Office, but when the war started, he was sent to the Peninsula with Military Intelligence and was attached to Sir Arthur's staff; he was to infiltrate the enemy lines and bring back what information he could. In fact, he was a spy for Lord Wellington and he became an expert at cracking the French military codes – I am not sure if you know that Papa is as fluent in French as in English, his mother is French.

'He was backwards and forwards between London, Spain and Portugal and had his base in Weymouth because of the easy crossing to Cherbourg . . .' She looked up at him and saw bewilderment in his face. 'What is it, Christopher?'

'But Caroline, all this is over five years ago – I know that because my brother, John, was at Talavera. You must have been no more than a child.'

She nodded. 'Yes, I was, but you see I had my Tante Michelle with me and Papa went backwards and forwards quite safely.'

'But what about Hatherley Park?'

Caroline hesitated. 'I was never told the whole story, but it was something to do with the Foreign Office.'

'And you stayed in Weymouth?'

'Yes, it is a mystery even to me. I was told that alterations were needed at Hatherley and I could go and live with Papa when they were finished. But this week, I have seen Hatherley and my cousin Thora – whom I do not like very much – and everything seems to be in order. But, Christopher, please be patient for we are getting nowhere. I have to tell you about Anna. You see, Papa is not ill, he has been caught as a spy in France and Pierre has taken Anna over there. She is posing as his wife to try and secure his release. I was sent here and I have heard nothing, that is why I worry.'

Christopher exploded with his next words. 'Dammit, I have never heard so much tarradiddle in all my days. It cannot be true.'

Caroline was near to tears and beat her hands against his chest. 'You must believe me, I would never lie to you, Christopher. I know I have lied about Papa being ill in Weymouth, but that was just for safety's sake. Papa is used to taking care of himself; it is Anna I am worried about, but what can I do?'

Christopher held her close, and thought hard. He did believe her and he must try to help her.

'Would you like me to go to Weymouth for you?'

She shook her head. 'It is kind indeed of you, Christopher, but I cannot involve you in our deceits. You are a clergyman. But I feel better already for having told you; I know that the true facts will be safe with you. What I would ask, and it may be asking too much, is if you would stay in West Wilton until I have news. It might be several days.'

'Of course I will do it, my sweet . . . no, do not protest – after we have had out luncheon, I will go and see Joshua who is my curate and arrange everything. Then I will take you back to Ponderfields and will stay at the rectory for as long as you need me. Oh, Caroline, not more tears, what have I said now?'

'You are so kind,' she sobbed, 'and I cannot say what I would like to say until I have seen Anna. Thank you, Christopher. I promise not to cry any more.'

But Caroline would have shed even more tears had she been at her father's side in Cherbourg. In spite of the drinks they were giving him and the cupping by *le médecin*, Philippe went from high fever and restless thrashing about, to shivering fits which would not go in spite of the many woollen blankets Mme. Barhard piled upon him.

By the fourth day, *le médecin* looked serious, and Anna went about with leaden feelings and a pit of sickness in her stomach. Pierre still insisted on taking her out when Mme. Barnard sat with the patient and one morning, Anna asked him to take her to the church.

Inside, she sat still and the only words which would come were 'Please don't let Philippe die.' She lit a candle for him at Pierre's instruction for it seemed a strange and Papist thing to do. But the little flame gave her some comfort as it burned in front of her; in her imagination, she thought of it rising to Heaven though she had always thought that Heaven was not in the sky, but any place where one might find peace at the last.

But there was no change in Philippe that day. *Le médecin* looked more serious than ever and kept shaking his head. The crisis came on the following day.

It was Anna's turn to sit with him and he was in one of his restless fits – she could pick out the same words. She knew now that it was Carrie; but an evil something, and a door, and the strange sounding salt were still beyond her understanding. She wiped his forehead with a cool cloth, keeping his long dark hair from falling into his eyes, and held his hand. Sometimes he would hold on to her fiercely, then would come the waving of the arms and the terrible twisting and turnings of his body.

He is not going to live, she would think, and in her heart she would cry, 'Philippe, Philippe, live for me, I love you.' And she knew now that it was true. Her feelings for Christopher could not approach the ferocity of the love which made her wish for Philippe to live.

Mme. Barnard crept into the room with fresh lemon and barley water and she, too, shook her head. 'He is bad, that one,' she said, and Anna saw her go from the room unable to stop the tears which trickled down her face.

Anna tried to get him to drink, but it was impossible; she got angry with him in her distress and shouted out loud. 'Philippe, you cannot die. It is Anna. Anna. And I love you.'

She watched as he went still and feared the worst. 'Anna, I love you,' he gasped.

And his head went back on the pillows and he was still. His face was grey and waxen but he looked peaceful.

Anna took a deep breath, got up from her chair and rushed from the room. 'Mme. Barnard, Mme. Barnard. It is the end. *Il est mort.*'

And Mme. Barnard came running from the kitchen making the sign of the cross and muttering a prayer. She ran up the stairs with Anna close behind her.

Philippe had not moved.

'*Le pauvre*,' said Mme. Barnard and took his wrist in her fingers feeling for his pulse.

Anna watched as the good woman's expression changed. 'Miss Anna, his pulse. You feel, it beats steady. Quick, you must feel.'

And while Anna tried to find the pulse, Mme. Barnard turned back the blankets and put her ear to his chest. She lifted her head and gave the broadest of smiles. 'He lives, Miss Anna, his heart is beating, look you can see he breathes peacefully. He is in good sleep now, no fever . . . oh, Miss Anna, do not cry.'

For Anna, putting her head to Philippe's chest could feel that he was breathing slowly and steadily. She sat down on the chair and burst into tears.

'I thought he was dead, Mme. Barnard, he was so white and still. Oh, thank you, *madame*, how can I thank you?' And she stood up and the two of them hugged each other. Then Anna ran downstairs to find Pierre.

Four hours later, Philippe came out of his deep sleep. Anna watched him open his eyes and look around him. He saw her looking there and gave a smile. 'Good God, Anna, what are you doing here. And where am I? I seemed to be having a nightmare and you were in it. Then you seemed to say 'I love you, Philippe' and the bad dream was over.'

'Hush, Philippe, do not talk. Please, have a drink. You have been very ill.'

'Not that damnable fever again? I never seem to know when I am going to get it. What day is it?'

'Saturday. Stop talking and go to sleep again.'

But he looked puzzled. 'Saturday? But, I remember now, I was in that lock-up and you came and they let me go. But that was at the beginning of the week.'

'You have been ill for four days, Philippe. But please have a drink and go to sleep. You have got to recover now.'

He took the drink from her and seemed glad of it, then he glanced around the room. 'This is the Barnards' room. Are we in Cherbourg?'

'Yes, we are.'

'Goddammit, Carrie will be wondering where we are.'

'Caroline is all right; do not worry about her.'

'No, I won't if you say so. You stay there and I will go to sleep again.'

It took four more days and a lot of Mme. Barnard's good food for Philippe to regain his strength. Anna was astonished at his quick recovery. He was downstairs on the second day and eager to talk to Anna.

'Did I let out any secrets when I was in the fever, Anna?'

'None at all. It was just the same as the last time at Hatherley Park. A whole lot of nonsense, and French which was so quick I could hardly understand a word. But, Philippe, the three words you kept repeating were the same.'

'What were they?' he asked lightly.

'It was something that was an evil and then a door, and salt, it didn't sound quite like salt but you kept saying it. It was on your mind, for both times I could pick out those words more than any others – except for Carrie, of course; I know about Caroline now. I told you that she is with my mama.'

She saw that his expression was puzzled; his face was no longer gaunt and white as it had been during his illness.

'An evil? A door? Salt?' he kept saying, and shaking his head. Then he gave a shout of laughter and Anna thought that it was good to hear it.

'No, it is not an evil or a door or salt,' he smiled at her. 'It is the Nivelle and the Adour, they are rivers near the Pyrenees; there was a battle of Nivelle and it was the French Marshal Soult who has been the head of the French Army. It was where I caught this fever for the first time. Pierre would have known for he was with me. I thought it was all up with me then, but he nursed me through it. Are you satisfied, young lady? Did you think that I was giving away military secrets?'

'No, I did not. At Hatherley, I had no idea of your spying activities. I did not think to ask Pierre.' She gave a laugh. 'To tell you the truth, I thought it must be something to do with your past life and that you had a guilty conscience.'

'I have no guilty conscience, I was an honourable spy and a good one. Did Carrie tell you? Or Pierre perhaps? it is one of life's little ironies that I was caught by the French on the one occasion I was not spying.'

'You really were going to see your mama in Paris?'

'Yes, I was. I had my orders from Lord Wellington to be on the move to Paris. As soon as I heard that Napoleon had abdicated and that King Louis was on the way to the capital, I knew that it was safe. And of course, I would be able to see mama as well; it is many years since I have seen her.' Philippe's attention wondered and she thought perhaps he was tired.

'You are talking too much, Philippe, you must not tire yourself,' she said quietly.

'Yes, ma'am,' he replied. 'But I have not yet thanked you for coming to my rescue. Now I will have to do some thinking. Do I continue to Paris, or do I take you back to England?'

TEN

ANNA LOOKED AT Philippe in horror. 'You cannot think of continuing to Paris. You have been very ill; I thought you had died . . . oh, Philippe,' she stumbled over her words.

He took her hand and she was surprised at the strength of his grasp. 'Would you have cared, Anna?'

She recovered herself quickly. 'Of course I would have cared. I nursed you all those days and I thought I had not saved you, do not remind me. But how can you think of going on to Paris? You need to rest. The last time, it was nearly four weeks before you were fit and strong again. And what about Caroline? I know that she is with my mama, but she will have had no word from you and she will be very worried. You must not forget that she does not even know that I succeeded in getting you from the prison.'

'Yes, you are right, *ma chère*, we will wait two days and then we will sail back to Weymouth. Now I will sleep.'

On the day before their return to England, Anna noticed a change come over Philippe. During the days following his recovery, he had been in what she thought of as a softer mood. They had talked a lot together; they had laughed together; he told her about Caroline, and Anna confided in him her hopes of Christopher and his daughter. This latter seemed both to please and amuse him.

After breakfast on their last day, Philippe appeared to be very serious and Anna thought that she noticed a slight return of his arrogant and what she thought of as his Mr Darcy look.

It was a fine day, but it was not quite into May and the wind was cool off the sea.

Philippe had dressed quite informally on the days after his illness, but that morning, he was attired in grey breeches and top boots, his dark-blue cutaway coat lightened by a cream waistcoat, his neckcloth as always impeccable. Anna thought that Pierre must have carefully carried and pressed his better clothes for when he hoped to present himself to Lord Wellington in Paris and to meet his mother.

'Anna,' Philippe said, as they walked into the living-room at the front of the house. There was no dining-room and they took their meals in the very large kitchen. 'I would like to walk as far as the harbour. Would you care to come?'

Anna thought it was spoken stiffly and wondered what had caused the change in him. Perhaps it is his illness, she said to herself, he must be feeling rather weak. 'Yes, I would like to come, thank you.' Then to counter the formal reply, she spoke again. 'Pierre took me out every morning while you were ill. I like it by the harbour.'

'I am glad to hear it.'

He said no more so she went upstairs for her pelisse and bonnet and joined him by the front door.

Neither was anything said during the short walk to the harbour and Anna decided that she must wait for Philippe to speak first. They walked as far as the end of the mole and she stood, as always, fascinated by the sea and the swirling currents.

'Anna, I have to talk to you about our situation.' It was if a stranger had spoken and when she looked up at him, the lines of his face seemed very strained. She did not know how to reply and simply nodded.

'First of all,' he continued 'I owe you a great debt of gratitude for being prepared to come over to France and to pose as my wife in order to secure my release. There are few young ladies of my acquaintance who would have agreed to such a venture, and you carried it out with courage and with a great sense of invention. And then I must thank you for nursing me; I owe it to you that I am standing here today.'

'Oh no,' Anna said hastily. 'It was your strong constitution which saved you. All I did was to sit by your bed and give you drinks. And you must not forget that Mme. Barnard shared the time with me.'

'No, I do not forget and I have thanked her and will repay her in some way. Both M. and Mme. Barnard have been good friends to me for a long time. But enough of the Barnards, it is you I must consider.'

'You have no need, sir, I did it all quite willingly and I am pleased that you are now free and well enough to return to England. Caroline will be pleased, too.' Anna spoke in a rush; she could feel a slight awkwardness between them, but could not make sense of it. Only the previous day, they had laughed together about her thinking that in his delirium, he had talked about salt when it was Marshal Soult he had had on his mind.

'I do not wish to speak about Carrie at the moment, she is safely with your mama. But your position in society has been compromised by your coming to my aid as my wife and staying with me during my illness. The only way I can redress the awkward situation you find yourself in, is by asking you to be my wife.'

Anna stared at him bewildered. This was never the Philippe who had kissed her so fiercely and so thankfully in the *gendarmerie*, the sick man who had responded when she had told him that she loved him, the cheerful but weak companion of the last few days.

I must be careful, she told herself, he feels he is under an obligation to me. 'Sir, I must thank you for your offer, but please do not feel that you are obliged to make it. I would never accept an offer of marriage made in such circumstances. I have never at any time this last week been on my own with you, not until this very moment. At the *gendarmerie*, Pierre was there, and since then there has always been M. or Mme. Barnard with us. Tomorrow we will be back in Weymouth and even if your sister has not returned, there will still be Pierre. You will have no need to think you have compromised me. After that, you can stay in Weymouth until you are fully recovered, or Pierre can drive us both back to West Wilton in the carriage. I have no doubt your cousin will be pleased to see you; Caroline will be overjoyed.'

Anna had kept talking to try and diffuse the tautness between them; she looked up and met his eyes as she finished speaking. His expression was steely, his manner emotionless. He is hiding something, she thought, he has not told me the whole truth about his work with the Foreign Office. And what does he do now that Napoleon is defeated and we have peace once again? I imagine he will marry his cousin and settle at Hatherley Park.

These thoughts caused her some heartbreak; in any other circumstances, and if he had professed any kind of love for her, it would have given her great joy to be married to him and to live at Hatherley. But to be his wife because he had felt obliged to ask her? No, it would never do.

Even as she had been thinking these sentiments, he had walked a few steps away from her and was staring into the waters at the end of the harbour wall. She did not move but stood and watched him; even though his head was slightly bent, his proud bearing, his square shoulders, his elegant strength were how she would always remember him. That is the true Mr Philippe Peverill, she said to herself.

He turned back to her. 'I have to say, ma'am, that your refusal of my offer has come as a great relief to me.'

She looked at him incredulously; was he so intent on marrying Thora? She spoke her thoughts. 'I imagine you are committed to your cousin; it would put you in a very embarrassing situation if I had accepted you, though I have to say that your offer was honourably made. It cannot have been easy for you.'

He stood looking down at her once again. 'I wish you to know that I have never made any commitment to my cousin; the supposed happy union between us existed solely in her imagination. My relief at your refusal is for quite another reason and it shames me to have to tell you of that reason. Now that my work at the Foreign Office will soon be officially over, I find myself a gentleman of no substance. If you had accepted my offer, the best with which I could have provided you, would have been a modest Foreign Office pension and a life in London, or in the very small house in Weymouth which belongs to my sister.' The next words were bitterly said. 'If and when I choose to marry, it will have to be to a wealthy heiress at the very least' He paused and then added, still with bitterness but tempered with a strange sorrow, 'There is only one lady I wish to have at my side for the rest of my life and that prospect is barred to me.'

Anna could not believe what she was hearing from him. This from the proud Mr Peverill? The owner of Hatherley Park?

'But . . . but, Mr Peverill . . .' Anna found herself stammering 'what about Hatherley Park?'

His voice was stern. 'Hatherley Park is not mine. I do not wish to discuss the matter further. If you would like to take my arm, I will escort you back to the Barnards' cottage.'

Anna was so amazed and stunned, that she hardly remembered walking back to the house. Then she went up to her room and could not stop thinking about the intelligence she had just received. She knew from Thora that Philippe had been profligate in his youth, but his ownership of Hatherley Park had implied that he was a wealthy man. It was yet another mystery of the personage of Mr Philippe Peverill and she had thought that she had learned all his secrets.

And the final irony, she smiled ruefully to herself, was that he had said that if he married at all, it would have to be to a wealthy heiress. She tried to imagine what his reaction would have been had she told him of her wealth, but she failed. She could only think that he would have regarded her with scorn – certainly not offered her the love she longed for.

Their return to Weymouth was uneventful, but they arrived at the house to find a very worried Tante Michelle.

'Philippe,' she cried, as he entered the house. 'You have returned at last. And this is Miss Anna Starkie? Did you indeed rescue him from prison? But why has it taken so long? No, do not explain. It is Caroline; why has she gone into Somerset with Dorcas? The maids have been telling me about it. I left her with Mrs Belcher, but Mrs Belcher says she has not seen Caroline. And our poor sister Marie, her eighth child and so pulled down with the fever. I returned yesterday and cannot tell you how glad I am to see you.'

Philippe was holding her hands. 'Michelle, calm down. This is not like you. I must first of all introduce you properly to Miss Starkie.' He turned to Anna. 'This is my dear sister Michelle, and she is not usually in such a worry about things. Now, we have a lot to talk about so we will all have a glass of wine and I will try and tell you everything that has happened, Michelle.'

So the tale was told, and Anna liked Tante Michelle – it was decided that she should call Philippe's elder sister by that name. Michelle could not believe that Philippe had also been in a fever and decided that it must be a family weakness.

But what pleased her most was that Caroline had been sent to Anna's mother; she laughed at Caroline and Dorcas on the stage-coach and told them that had she not been in such a worry about Philippe and Marie, she, too would have enjoyed the journey on the stage when she travelled to London.

They tried to persuade Philippe to rest a few days in Weymouth, but he would have none of it, and the journey to Somerset was planned for the next day.

Anna was both relieved and amused to hear him talking so cheerfully with his sister and hoped that the strained conversation and decisions at Cherbourg were a thing of the past.

They travelled north the next day, arriving at Ponderfields in the middle of the afternoon.

The carriage had been heard on the gravel of the drive, and Philippe and Anna got down to find a wildly excited Caroline running towards them.

'Papa, you are safe. And, Anna, you found him? Did they keep you as well? Where have you been all this time, I have been in such a worry? I do not know what I would have done if Christopher had not stayed with me – oh, here he is. Christopher, they are both here safe and sound.'

There were kisses and hugs for everyone and Christopher kissed Anna on the cheek and shook hands with Philippe. They all went indoors and the excitement was renewed when Mrs Starkie came to greet them.

'Anna, it is good to have you home again. Are you quite recovered, Mr Peverill? I hope that Anna took good care of you.'

Philippe, surprisingly, took Mrs Starkie's hands in his. 'She is a very good girl, your daughter, Mrs Starkie, and I thank you for letting her come to me. I must also thank you for having Carrie to stay with you; it was indeed very kind and provided me with much relief that she was safely here. It is good to see Christopher here, too, that will have been a great comfort to her, I am sure.' He looked round at them all. 'And now I must continue to Hatherley Park, I know that my cousin will have been anxious for news of me. Carrie, I will come and fetch you tomorrow. Now, I will bid you all good-day.'

Anna watched him leave the room. He did not even look at her, but headed straight for the carriage and was driven off. It is almost as though he has walked from my life, she thought sadly, yet I will see him again for Hatherley is very near to us. Now I must concentrate on making sure that Christopher and Caroline come to some agreement. I can sense a happiness between them even though I have not yet spoken to them. They are trying to avoid looking at each other which must signify something.

She made sure of having a private word with Christopher before he left for the rectory.

But before that, and while Anna was taking her things up to her bedroom, Christopher managed to take Caroline on one side; Mrs Starkie had gone upstairs with Anna.

'Caroline, I am so happy for you. I do not understand about the fever, but I expect you will have the whole story from Anna. Your papa certainly looks as though he has been ill, but you must be glad to see him again.' He noticed that she had gone quiet and thought he could guess her thoughts. 'Caroline, I must be on my way back to Battiscombe tomorrow, but I will come and see you before I set off. I want you to know that I am still of the same mind about us. I do understand your feelings, but please remember that I love you and want to marry you. I shall see your father and ask his permission to address you, for that is the correct way. That all sounds very formal and I do not mean to be formal with you. So please smile at me now that you can smile again, and I will kiss you goodbye, if I may.'

Caroline felt that she had two hearts; one which told her to say yes to Christopher and the other which said that she must make sure of Anna's feelings now that she was home again.

I love you, Christopher, she wanted to say, but dare not. So instead, she put her hands out to him and stood on tip-toe so that she could kiss him on the cheek.

He gave her a hug in return. 'That was very nice Caroline. Thank you. I will see you tomorrow.'

Next morning, Anna and Caroline were walking in the garden when Christopher arrived. He was in the gig.

'Good morning, young ladies,' he said cheerfully. 'It pleases me to be able to say that. I have brought the gig as I thought we might drive over to Hatherley Park. I wish to see your papa, as you know, Caroline, and I expect you will want to arrange your return either to Weymouth or to Hatherley.' He went up to Anna. 'You continually refused to marry me, Anna, and I have now lost my heart to Caroline. She, also, refuses me because she thinks you are bound to me; I am trusting that when I return to Battiscombe later today, that you will speak to her in my favour. And Anna, I wish you success with *Mr Darcy*.'

He kissed her on the cheek and they both laughed.

Caroline was indignant. 'You are talking nonsense, both of you. *Mr Darcy* is in *Pride and Prejudice*, even I know that.'

Anna smiled. 'I will tell you when Christopher has gone back to Battiscombe. I think I can guess why he wants to see your papa.'

They told Mrs Starkie where they were going and she seemed pleased; she had seen Caroline and Christopher together and expected a happy outcome; she also had hopes of Anna and Mr Philippe Peverill of Hatherley Park. Although she had insisted to Caroline that Anna was attached to Christopher, she had not failed to notice the expression in her daughter's eyes when Mr Peverill was in the room.

At Hatherley, they were admitted by a distressed Mrs Shapter.

'Oh please do come along in, Miss Caroline. Such trouble and I don't know how to tell you, I'm sure ... and Miss Anna and Mr Christopher, oh please come in the drawing-room.'

Christopher spoke for them all. 'Is Mr Peverill unwell again?'

'He has gone.' It was all Mrs Shapter managed to say and they stared at her.

Anna spoke kindly to her. 'Sit down, Mrs Shapter ... no, it does not matter if it is the drawing-room. Please try and tell us.'

'It were yesterday when Mr Peverill returned and Miss Peverill that glad to see him. A letter was here for him, very official-looking, it were, from London; it came a few days back. Well, I don't know what was in the letter, but it must have been that important because he came into the kitchen where Shapter and me was talking with that manservant of Mr Peverill's and he said, I mean Mr Peverill, said to Pierre to go and help pack up their belongings because they had to go away quick. And we all helped and loaded up the carriage and first thing this morning with only a cup of tea for their breakfast, they was off. It must have been about five o'clock and Shapter thinks as how they took the Bath road and it was ... oh, lordy me, I did forget. Mr Peverill gave me a note to give to you, Miss Caroline. He said as he was sure you would come today but if not, for Shapter to take it over to Ponderfields. And that's all. They've gone, the pair of them, and I don't know where and I don't know why for it's none of my business, but it seems strange to me them rushing off like that and Miss Peverill as well and Mr Peverill only just on the mend from that nasty fever and—'

It was Caroline who seemed to recover her senses the most quickly. 'Mrs Shapter, have you got the note which Papa left for me?'

Mrs Shapter jumped up. 'Oh, miss, I'm sorry, I were quite forgetting. It's on the table in the hall; I'll fetch it for you.'

The note was brought and Mrs Shapter remembered her place and went back to the kitchen while Caroline opened it.

The other two had been shocked into silence and both watched Caroline's face. Anna thought that whatever the message was, it had not upset the young girl.

'It's all right, Anna, I will read it aloud for it is nothing secret or personal though we are not very much the wiser . . . there is one thing I do not understand though.'

My dear Carrie
I am sorry but I have been called away to London on urgent business. Thora is coming with me; we will not be returning to Hatherley Park. Please ask Mrs Starkie if she will kindly have you at Ponderfields until I can come for you.
    Your loving Papa
            Philippe Peverill

Caroline gave it to Anna who read it and passed it to Christopher; both of them frowned slightly.

'Why does he say that he will not be returning to Hatherley Park?' Christopher asked the all-important question.

The two girls shook their heads. 'That is what I do not understand, there is no explaining it,' said Caroline. 'You do not suppose that they have gone up to London to get married, do you? They could live in the London house.'

Anna felt a sinking of the heart at the thought of Thora and Philippe being man and wife, but then she remembered something else and looked at the two others. 'Philippe did tell me when we were in Cherbourg – oh, I am sorry – Christopher does not know about Cherbourg—'

Caroline interrupted hastily. 'Christopher knows everything, Anna. I am sorry, I know that it was all meant to be secret, but I was so worried when you did not return, that I told him everything. He was such a comfort to me.'

Anna smiled. 'You did right, Caroline, and now I can speak quite openly. Philippe told me that he would be in straightened circumstances now that his work with the Foreign Office was finished; he implied that his only income would be a small pension. Perhaps he could no longer afford to live at Hatherley. I can understand that, but not why both of them had to go at crack of dawn without even saying goodbye to you. Does it upset you, Caroline?'

Caroline managed a laugh. 'I am so used to Papa's sudden comings and goings that it does not surprise me. But I still do not want to have Thora as my new mama; there is something about her I do not like though I cannot explain it to you.'

They all talked and each of them made wild suggestions and it ended with them laughing about the affair, and Christopher returning to Battiscombe.

After Christopher had left them, Anna and Caroline found that they had a lot to talk about. It was now early in May and they found it delightful to have each other's company as they walked in the Ponderfields' gardens or further afield to the Hatherley wood. It was an especially nice place to be, with oaks, elms and larches clothed in that fresh new green which is only seen in the spring.

They had found a fallen tree and it became a habit with them to walk across the fields, sit together on the log and enjoy each other's company.

Anna did her best to find out whether Caroline cared for Christopher and if she had been right in thinking that he had been seeking an interview with Philippe in order to ask permission to address himself to Caroline.

'Did Christopher take good care of you while I was away, Caroline?'

'He came every day without fail. He was astonished that I did not ride, but he took me around to see the district in his gig. We even went into Bath, which was most interesting, except that he made me try the mineral waters. Have you tasted them, Anna?'

Anna laughed. 'Only once,' she replied. 'I was quite small and I was sure that I was being poisoned. I think they are more beneficial to those valetudinarians who go to the actual baths. If they did no good, Bath would not be such a successful spa town.'

'I enjoyed the visit to Battiscombe best of all,' said Caroline innocently.

'Christopher took you to Battiscombe?' Anna felt that this augured well and wanted to hear more.

'Yes, it is not an old church, but the vicarage is a lovely old building.'

'And you would like it to be your home, Caroline?' Anna saw the red colour flush the young girl's face and guessed that she would soon know the truth.

'Anna, you must not say such things. You know very well that it was always planned that Christopher should marry you. Your mama told me about it.'

'And did she tell you that I have always refused him when he asked me to marry him?' Anna spoke quietly.

Caroline nodded and then smiled. 'Yes, she said that you were a naughty girl and that she looked forward to having Christopher as a son-in-law.'

'Mama is quite wrong,' replied Anna decidedly.

'What do you mean, Anna?'

'I shall never marry Christopher. I am fond of him but no more than that. I was so sure that you and he would suit and I believe that I am right. Tell me,' she demanded.

Caroline flushed again. 'You put it in that *post scriptum* to his mama,' she accused Anna. 'You were match-making, you cannot deny it.'

Anna smiled. 'Yes, I was match-making. Have I succeeded, Caroline?'

'No, you have not,' was the emphatic reply from Caroline.

'You mean that you do not love him?'

Anna loved the confusion in Caroline's face, knowing that she was very near to the truth of the matter.

Caroline decided to be honest. 'I will tell you because you are my friend. I do love Christopher – it happened straight away, Anna, just like that.'

'I thought it would. And Christopher took you to Battiscombe to show you the vicarage and to ask you to marry him?' asked Anna, secretly amused.

'You are asking a lot of questions,' replied Caroline. 'But I will tell you the truth, Anna. Christopher did ask me to marry him and I refused.'

It was just as I thought, said Anna to herself, now I must find out why. 'I do not understand. If you say you love Christopher and I can tell he loves you, why did you refuse him?'

Caroline turned to face Anna. 'You must know why. How could I accept Christopher when your mama expects you to marry him? I could not say yes to him knowing that, could I, Anna?'

'You are a good friend, Caroline, and it was very loyal of you, but I will tell you a secret. I could never marry Christopher. I love someone else.'

Caroline tried to read Anna's expression. 'You. . . .?' Then her face broke into smiles. 'You love Papa. I can guess, I am right, please tell me I am right, Anna. And it was what Christopher meant, was it not? Do you call my papa *Mr Darcy*? I can guess why, sometimes he can look very proud and haughty, just as I imagine Mr Darcy to have looked. But Papa is not really like that, you know, he is very loving and caring. Do you love him, Anna?'

'Yes, I do love Philippe, but it is hopeless and now he has probably gone off and married Thora.'

'Never; he would never marry Thora if he loved you,' said his daughter, outraged.

'But he does not love me, Caroline.'

'How do you know? Has he asked you to marry him? I demand you tell me the truth.' Anna had never seen Caroline so persistent before.

So she had to tell the story of the proposal on the harbour at Cherbourg. Caroline was indignant. 'He is foolish, my papa, he should have swept you into his arms and told you that he loved you.'

Anna laughed and laughed. 'Caroline, you are the dearest of girls, but you must realize that maybe he really does not love me. And do not ever repeat this conversation to your papa, will you?'

'No, I promise, but I shall try and help things along. Though how I can do that if you are here and we are back in Weymouth or even in London, I cannot imagine. I wish I knew about the mystery of Hatherley Park and why he and Thora had to rush off so secretly.'

They were soon to find out, but it was only after several days of idle speculation between the two of them and then the arrival of a strange and surprising letter.

ELEVEN

It was ten o'clock in the morning and Anna and Caroline, having breakfasted late, were to be found still at the breakfast-table deciding where their walk should take them that day. Neither of them was in cheerful mood for they still awaited news of Caroline's papa. Days had gone by since his sudden disappearance from Hatherley and they were still at a loss to understand it.

A maid came into the dining-room with a letter which, she told them, had just been sent up from the Letter Receiving Office in the village. Anna went upstairs to fetch the amount owing on the letter and gave it to the maid.

The two girls took it into the drawing-room with some curiosity, and an unexpected beating of the heart on behalf of Anna as she thought that it might be from Philippe

They looked at it together when they found that it was directed to *Miss Anna Starkie and Miss Caroline Peverill.* It did not seem to be a man's hand, the writing being rather sprawling and flowery.

'Oh, I was hoping that it would be from Papa but that is not his hand; he writes very neatly,' said Caroline. 'Open it quickly, Anna.'

They broke the seal and spread the sheet of paper flat, there were but few words on it. But those words kept their eyes riveted to the letter in front of them as though in total disbelief.

No 8 Trim Street
Bath

My dear Anna and Caroline
You will be surprised to receive this from me, but I have much news to impart and I would like you to join me for luncheon this coming Saturday here in Bath. I hope that you will have the use of the Ponderfields' carriage and I look forward to seeing you. Trim Street is just round the corner from the Theatre Royal.
With kindest regards
Thora

Then Anna read it again, out loud this time, and they both looked at each other.

'Does it mean she has married Papa and that they are in Bath?' said Caroline, and Anna thought she sounded fearful.

'I do not know,' she replied. 'But I am inclined to think not, unless Philippe has let Thora write the invitation. *I have news to impart* could mean anything. We will not think the worst, Caroline, but try and be patient until Saturday comes. I will go and show it to Mama and ask her if we can have the carriage. I am assuming that you would like to go?'

Caroline smiled wanly. 'I must try not to imagine what might have happened, but I cannot help wishing that we could hear from Papa. I wonder if he is with Thora?'

Saturday came all too slowly, but when it did come, they were both of them glad that it was a fine day and they could wear pretty summer dresses.

Anna knew Bath well, but it was only Caroline's second visit;

they passed the Pump Room and the Abbey, soon the Theatre Royal was in sight and Trim Street easily found.

George-Coachman helped them down from the carriage and knocked at the door of No 8 for them.

A maid-servant answered and showed them into a small drawing-room at the front of the house. Here Thora stood, quite resplendent and both Anna and Caroline gazed at her in utter astonishment

Gone was the spartan and circumspect Miss Thora Peverill of Hatherley Park and in her place, but with the same tall, domineering personality was a woman who could only be described in Anna's fleeting, shocked imagination as a woman of the town. Thora was dressed in a gaudy purple satin which was bordered at the hem and neckline with what seemed to be swansdown, and the neck was cut so low that the swansdown barely covered the full curve of her ample breasts. She held a fan and her curls, in spite of being indoors, were powdered and topped with a head-dress of plumes and ribbons, also in purple.

This vision who indeed was Thora, spoke in what could only be described as coarse accents. 'Oh la, my dears, how very nice of you to come to my modest abode, I am charmed, indeed I am. Now do sit down and Becky will bring us some wine and we will have a nice little coze before it is time for luncheon which is quite simple for when I am at home – it is not very often, I must say – I eat very sparingly in order to enjoy the fine dinners I have partaken of since I have been in Bath. Now what was you saying, Caroline? And I have not asked after your dear, dear papa, *mon cher* Philippe I call him for I love him to distraction. You are a lucky girl to have such a handsome and charming father . . .'

Anna could stand it no longer. 'Thora, are you married to Mr Peverill?'

'Married to Philippe? Whatever made you think such a thing?

As though Mr Philippe Peverill would marry an actress like myself. No, no, he looks much higher, I am sure of that.'

Caroline looked at Anna, an appealing look which said, please, Anna, you deal with this awful woman for I am sure I cannot.

Anna understood nothing and it was obvious that Thora was playing a part with them. But why? And was she really an actress? She certainly looked and behaved like one.

'Thora.' Anna decided to be forthright. 'Caroline has not had a single word from her papa. That is why, on receiving your letter, we thought he might be with you in Bath. But it seems not. Are you really an actress? You certainly look like one. And what has happened to Miss Thora Peverill.'

Thora beamed at them. 'It is nice of you to come for I hope that I can do a little explaining. Please be prepared for a long story.

Thora's stories are always long, thought Anna irreverently.

'Now, my dears, I must tell you that I am indeed an actress and I pride myself on being a very good one. I have been invited to play Mrs Malaprop in *The Rivals* here in Bath and at the Theatre Royal, too. In London, I number Lady Macbeth as one of my greatest interpretations. So I somehow think that I was made for the part of Miss Thora Peverill ... yes, my dear Caroline, you were going to say something?'

Caroline did not know whether to look delighted or not, but nothing could stop her questions. 'Do you mean, Thora, that you are not a Peverill? Not Papa's cousin? And that you are not going to marry him?'

Thora gave what could only be described as a vulgar roar of laughter. 'Me a Peverill? Do I look like a Peverill this morning? No, Caroline ... and Anna ... I am plain Thora Hazzard, well known on the London stage and now to tread the boards in Bath. It will be delightful. But I must answer your questions properly, for you took me in dislike, didn't you? Not good enough for your papa, and there was I thinking that I had played an excellent part as Miss Peverill—'

Anna interrupted. 'You did play it well, Thora, even if we do not know why, but once or twice you would say something that I considered, at the least, shabby-genteel. We accepted that you were Mr Peverill's cousin without question, but it seemed to pose a puzzle. In fact, everything has been a puzzle.'

'Oh la, Anna, and there was I thinking I had played the part to perfection. But I had to make it up as I went along. I knew what *cher* Philippe was about so I tried to disguise things by spreading tales of his goings on in Weymouth. I had met Caroline and Tante Michelle, but it amused me to put it about that Philippe was visiting his mistress when he went away. The village gossips loved it, didn't they?'

'I did not believe the gossip, Thora,' replied Anna. 'And then, of course, I met Caroline and discovered the truth.'

'I was sorry that *cher* Philippe was ill again. You were a good girl to go and nurse him as you had done at Hatherley Park. It was very nice to see him recovered last week.'

Anna glanced at Caroline and knew that both had the same thoughts. Thora had known nothing of Philippe's imprisonment or of Anna's excursion to France.

'You convinced us completely, Thora,' said Anna. 'I think you must be a very clever actress. But why did you and Philippe leave so hastily? And why were you at Hatherley in the first place?'

Thora was subdued for the first time. 'I will try and tell you exactly for some of it I do not understand myself and I was not allowed to ask questions. I had just finished playing Lady Teazle at Drury Lane when I was approached by someone from the Foreign Office. He asked if I was a discreet person who could act a part without asking questions; I told him that I hoped I was. So this is what he asked me, I remember almost exactly for he was very precise. A gentleman from the Foreign Office was assisting Lord Wellington in the Peninsular Campaign – he did not use the word spy – I found that out later when Philippe explained his absences – but I must not lose the point. The part they wanted me to play was that of housekeeper at Hatherley Park and also to be cousin to Mr Philippe Peverill. The remuneration was excellent and I could not refuse, the mystery of it also appealed. I met Mr Peverill and we knew we would suit, so from then on I was Miss Thora Peverill, Philippe's cousin. Then we moved to Hatherley Park—'

Caroline could not stop herself breaking in. 'But, Thora, I never understood why Papa moved to Hatherley. I accepted that you were our cousin, though I confess to not liking you very much. I thought you domineering and that you had designs on Papa. I could never understand why he could not continue his activities from Weymouth as he had done all those years. Do you know why it was?'

Thora was shaking her head and directed a kindly expression towards Caroline. 'No, my dear girl, it was never explained to me and I just had to accept it. Philippe knew, but did not take me into his confidence; in fact, he was always very formal with me when we were on our own. But I have to admit that I enjoyed playing the part and I consider that it was one of my best performances. You never guessed, did you, my dearies?'

Anna and Caroline began to chuckle and then Thora joined in until they were all convulsed with hearty laughter and all talking at once of their remembrances.

Caroline suddenly became solemn. 'But, Thora, do you know where Papa is now? Have you had word from him?'

Thora shook her head. 'Nothing; he brought me to Bath, found this nice little house for me, said thank you, goodbye, and set off for London. Why we had to do a sudden flit, I shall never know.

So if you find out, perhaps you will write and tell me. I would apprehend – oh, there I am doing a Mrs Malaprop already, I have been learning my lines, you know – I should have said that I would appreciate it very much if you would write to me.' She looked at them both. 'I tried to do some match-making while I was at Hatherley and I am sure you will do nicely for *mon cher* Philippe, Anna, and of course, Caroline and Christopher. Have you any news, my love?' This last directed at Caroline who shook her head and made no reply. 'There is time, there is time. Now let us partake of our luncheon and we will enjoy a laugh at the part I played so well at Hatherley Park.'

They did enjoy their meal and they said goodbye to a glowing Thora whom they thought that they might never see again unless they were to go to the play in Bath.

On the journey back to West Wilton, they did not stop talking once and could only admire Thora for all her efforts.

On the Monday after this historic visit to Bath, Caroline's mind was at last put at rest by the arrival of a letter from her father.

My dearest Carrie

I am sorry that an urgent letter from London caused me to rush away so quickly and without seeing you, though I did have time to leave a note for you with Mrs Shapter. I am hoping that Thora might have been in touch with you, although she did not know the reason for my sudden recall to London.

I am still held in London, but I am very well and hope to be with you in a few days.

Please give my kindest regards and sincere thanks to Mrs Starkie and, of course, to Anna.

Your devoted Papa

Philippe Peverill

Caroline ran to find Anna and the two of them read the letter again.

'He is just held up in London, Anna, that is all. I had been afraid that he might have been sent to the continent again, though I could not understand why. I saw it in your mama's morning paper that Lord Wellington had been invited by Lord Castlereagh to take the British Embassy in Paris, he has become the Duke of Wellington.'

Anna had a sudden thought. 'Do you think it is possible that your papa has been asked to take a post at the embassy? It would be an honour; he has his mother in Paris and, of course, he speaks fluent French. Would you like to live in Paris, Caroline?' She said it very deliberately and once again saw the tell-tale flush on Caroline's cheeks.

'No, I do not think I would,' replied Caroline hastily. 'I will always think of the French as the enemy, though I suppose that is wrong of me. As long as Napoleon is alive, even though he is in exile on Elba, he still seems as a threat to peace. I suppose, one day when Papa is home again, I will really believe that the Peninsular War is over. There are times when I have felt that I have taken part in it myself.' She looked at Anna not knowing quite what to expect after her little outburst, 'You can laugh at me if you like, but it has been a worrying time, never knowing when Papa was going to come home – indeed, if he was going to come home at all.'

Anna nodded in sympathy for she had been brought up in a happy family even after her papa had died. But Caroline was only eighteen and had never known a normal family life. 'You will feel better when your papa is here, Caroline.'

But later that day, Anna took it into her own hands to hasten the match between Christopher and Caroline and wrote a short note to summon him to West Wilton. It is time, she told herself, that he and Caroline were brought together.

Dear Christopher

I am writing to ask if you could come over for the day. We have surprising news of Philippe and Thora and not what we expected. It is too much to put in a note. But I do think I am right in saying that Caroline will be very pleased to see you.

Always your dear friend

Anna

She sent one of the stable boys over to Battiscombe that very day and next morning, she confidently awaited Christopher's arrival.

It was a dull morning but it was not cold; Anna told Caroline she had a headache and did not want to walk that morning.

'Would you like to go with Miss Swinburne?' Anna asked Caroline, knowing very well that she would receive a refusal. 'No, I will stay with you, Anna, but I will not chatter. Then later on, if you are feeling better, we can walk quietly round the garden. I am reading Miss Burney's novel *Cecilia* which I found in the library, so you can tell I will be quiet.'

They were quiet for over half an hour and Anna felt herself getting fidgety. It was nearly midday and there was no sign of Christopher, she had been so sure that he would come. It was just as they were finishing luncheon that Anna heard the sound of the door knocker at the front door, and when the maid opened the door and there was the sound of a male voice, she knew that it was Christopher.

Anna took Caroline's arm and they joined Christopher in the drawing-room where he was already talking to Mrs Starkie.

'Anna, Caroline,' he said, giving each of them his hand. 'I had to come over to see Father this morning and I could not return to Battiscombe without calling in to greet you.'

His eyes met Anna's and she gave a slight nod unseen by

Caroline. 'Will you both walk in the garden with me? It is not sunny, but at least it is mild.'

'Thank you, Christopher, but I will decline, if you will excuse me. I have had a headache all morning, but I am sure that Caroline would enjoy a breath of air.' Anna spoke quietly and sensibly and left Christopher to do the persuading.

'Caroline?' he questioned and Caroline could hear a soft encouragement in his voice.

'Thank you, Christopher, it would be very nice. Are you sure you will not come, Anna?'

'No, I would rather stay quiet if you do not mind. But you must not forget to tell Christopher of our visit to Bath,' replied Anna.

Caroline smiled, relieved not to have a romantic encounter thrust upon her. 'I will fetch my shawl,' she said. 'It is not quite warm enough to go out without one.'

The garden at Ponderfields was not long, but at the end there was an orchard; already some of the fruit trees were bearing their pretty pink and white blossom.

Christopher was smiling. 'This takes me back to when we were children and we used to pay hide-and-seek or tag around the trees. Ponderfields always seemed more exciting than the rectory.' He led her to a rough wooden bench which had no back to it. 'Would you like to sit down, Caroline? What is all this about a trip to Bath? Did you and Anna go shopping?'

'No, not at all, it was something quite different and I think you will find it hard to believe. We went to see Thora.'

'Thora? But I thought she had gone to London with her cousin.'

'He is not her cousin.'

'But they are both Peverills?'

'No, she is not a Peverill,' said Caroline, and knew she had started badly.

Christopher turned to look at her and took both her hands in his. 'You are not making any sense, young lady. Start at the very beginning and tell me the whole from start to finish.'

So Caroline told him the story and there were many interruptions and expressions of *Goddammit* and *Good God* from Christopher.

'I have now received a letter from Papa,' she concluded. 'I am expecting him any day now, maybe even tomorrow.'

Christopher was shaking his head. 'It is hard to credit Thora with playing such a role. She must be an excellent actress for she succeeded in taking us all in.' He gave a hearty laugh. 'And to think we thought that she was setting her cap at your papa; she certainly fooled us.' He was quiet for a second. 'But, Caroline, there is still the mystery of why they came to Hatherley Park in the first place. You still do not know?'

Caroline shook her head. 'No, nothing. Anna and I have thought and thought, but we get nowhere. Have you any ideas?'

'No, I don't think I have unless it is something to do with the Foreign Office. It sounds to me as though the letter summoning your papa to London must have been from his superiors, presumably Lord Castlereagh, for Philippe went off so suddenly and without even seeing you.' He lifted her hands to his lips. 'I have a mind to send a messenger to Battiscombe to say that I am detained for a day or two. I will wait until Philippe arrives and solves all the mysteries for us. I want to see him particularly in any case.'

Caroline had been so wrapped up in her tale that she had forgotten that Christopher had wanted an interview with her papa. He wanted permission to ask her to marry him which she thought was nonsense, because he had already asked her in her father's absence and she had refused him.

She was aware of her own feelings of love for him and she now knew of Anna's confession of love for Philippe. But how could a young lady of eighteen say such things to a clergyman four years older than herself?

Christopher, too was uncertain. He had been refused once and felt that the moment was awkward even though Anna had seemed to give him the hint that all was well.

With both of them absorbed in their own thoughts, they had not noticed the arrival on the scene of Miss Swinburne with Felicity, Selina and Jane. As usual, they threw themselves on Christopher with some excitement.

'Christopher, fancy you being here, and Caroline, too.' Felicity always took the lead for she was the eldest at fourteen years of age and described by her mother as a tomboy. 'We have come to play hide-and-seek as the orchard is a good place. Do you remember when you used to play with us when we were little? Please come and join us.' She was tugging at his hand. 'And Caroline.'

Miss Swinburne was obliged to rebuke Felicity; she secretly thought that she was a lively and engaging young girl who needed only firm management. 'Felicity, your behaviour is unladylike, you will have to learn better manners than that.'

Felicity liked Miss Swinburne and took heed of her; so she turned to Caroline and said quite prettily. 'I am sure that you will enjoy a game of hide-and-seek, Caroline, we promise not to be too rough. Or would you prefer to sit and talk to Christopher?'

At that moment, talking to Christopher was the last thing Caroline wanted and she got up obligingly, turning to Christopher as she did so. 'Shall we, Christopher? It will be fun to be quite young again. Does a clergyman play hide-and-seek?'

He grinned at her. 'This clergyman does; who is going to be "it" first?'

'You are,' chorused all the girls. 'Turn your head to that tree and count to a hundred and don't forget to keep your eyes shut.'

Many moments of fun followed with a lot of running about and shrieks of laughter. Even Miss Swinburne joined in and when it was her turn to hide her eyes and count to a hundred, Christopher, who was watching Caroline, saw her run behind a very tall laurel hedge which bordered one side of the orchard.

Caroline was standing out of sight when suddenly she found Christopher at her side. He was laughing.

'Caught you,' he said.

She was indignant. 'But you are not "it". Miss Swinburne will be hunting for us in a minute.'

'A minute is long enough for me to tell you that I love you and, please, will you marry me?'

'Christopher, you cannot ask me to marry you in the middle of a game of hide-and-seek.' Caroline was also laughing.

'I could not ask you while we were sitting on the bench, it has taken all that running about to give me the courage.'

'Oh, Christopher, what will you say next?'

'I will ask you if you love me, and what about Anna?'

She looked at him shyly. 'I have loved you from the beginning and I would like to marry you. I think I am supposed to thank you for your offer. I have talked to Anna. She was right to refuse you; she loves Papa, you know, but she does not know his thoughts or feelings. She had always thought he was looking to Thora, but now we know that is not true ... Christopher!' Her voice was raised in a shriek for he had taken her in his arms and kissed her fiercely.

'I deserve a kiss,' he said, his hands still round her slim waist. 'I love you and you love me, and you like Battiscombe so we can marry soon and live happily ever after. Of course, I still have to ask your Papa. Do you think he will object to you marrying the Vicar of Battiscombe?'

'Christopher, it is no use asking Papa when we have already decided it between ourselves. You have made me very happy.' And

Caroline reached up to kiss him on the cheek just as Miss Swinburne appeared through the gap in the hedge and immediately looked horrified.

'Caroline! Christopher! What is this behaviour all about? It is no good example to my girls . . . Christopher . . .' Miss Swinburne, of all people, gave a high-pitched giggle for Christopher had kissed the governess on the cheek.

'You are the first to know, Miss Swinburne. Caroline has agreed to become my wife.'

'But have you asked permission of her papa?' asked the very proper Miss Swinburne.

'Mr Peverill is in London,' Christopher replied. 'We expect him at any time and I will be able to approach him then. But, Miss Swinburne, you have found us, so you must go and seek the children out or they will be running to the tree which is "home" before you get there.'

'You are quite right, Christopher, but you must let me say that I am very pleased for both of you. I can see by your faces that you are very happy.'

She hurried off and Christopher took Caroline into his arms and kissed her again. 'Are you happy, my love?' he asked her.

'Very happy, thank you, Christopher.'

Back at Ponderfields, Anna had been equally happy because she had manoeuvred Christopher and Caroline into a walk together. It was worth pretending the headache, she told herself; now I think I deserve a walk, but I will go in the opposite direction.

So it was that early in the afternoon found Anna walking in the fields at the front of Ponderfields towards the Hatherley wood. She never ventured in that direction without remembering her first meeting with Philippe. It seems such a long time ago, she thought, and there is still so much I do not know about him, though I do

174

know that I love him. It may be a hopeless love, but if I have succeeded in bringing Caroline and Christopher together, I shall feel happy.

She entered the wood, thinking about Caroline with a great deal of satisfaction. That morning, Anna was wearing a morning-dress of pale cream sarsenet, embellished at the neckline with a fringe of a very deep blue. Her Norwich shawl was draped around her elbows and she let it stay, for on that May morning, even though she was under the trees, she was not cold.

She was lost in a fantasy of being in the West Wilton church at Christopher and Caroline's wedding, and when she came out of the daydream, she was startled to see the figure of a gentleman approaching her from the direction of Hatherley. She stopped in bewilderment, as though this moment had happened before. Coming towards her, was Mr Philippe Peverill.

TWELVE

Anna stood still as Philippe walked towards her. He was smiling and looked quite unlike the gentleman she had met on that first occasion and had thought of as Mr Darcy.

'Anna, my love,' he said as he took her hands.

She ignored the endearment. 'Philippe, you are home. I was just thinking as you walked along that you no longer looked like Mr Darcy.'

'And what is that remark supposed to mean?'

'The first time we met, you were so proud and disagreeable that I thought you were just like Mr Darcy in *Pride and Prejudice*. Have you read it?'

'I have and I hope you think I have changed just as Mr Darcy changed,' he said, as he looked down at her, a quizzical smile about his eyes.'

'Yes, when I saw you coming, I was struck by the difference in you,' she replied.

'I thank you, ma'am. I hope you noticed the expression of *heartfelt delight* which must have shown in my face when I saw you approaching. I say that just to prove that I have read the book, of course.'

She ignored this last remark, feeling that the conversation was becoming excessively sentimental. 'You have come straight from London, sir?'

'I have, and on my arrival at Hatherley Park, my first thought was to walk over to Ponderfields to see you and Carrie. You are alone?'

'Yes, I am,' she replied, and then wondered if she should not give some clue as to Caroline's whereabouts. 'I came on my own because I wished to leave Christopher and Caroline to walk in the Ponderfields' gardens together.'

'Are you match-making?' he demanded. 'I thought it was you who was attached to Christopher.'

She chuckled. 'Only by our respective mamas in our babyhood. Would you approve of a match between Caroline and Christopher?'

He did not hesitate. 'I would indeed. It would save me having to give her a season in London to catch a husband.'

'Philippe!' Anna was outraged.

'Ah, I am pleased to be able to shock you. I was coming to Ponderfields not only to see how Carrie was and to tender my thanks to your mama, but to plead my cause with you. I am glad to have met you here in the wood; it seems appropriate, for as you have reminded me, it was where we first met.'

Anna ignored the important part of this statement so that she could start her questioning. 'But, Philippe, where have you been and why did you disappear so suddenly? Oh, and Philippe, Caroline and I went to see Thora. She told us her story and we were vastly amused and think her a very fine actress. We thought that you were going to marry her.'

'No, it was never my intention. It was Thora who put it about, the wicked woman, it was not part of the plan at all, but she played it so well.' He stopped and looked at her. 'Anna, my dear, there is a lot of explaining to do, but most of it, I need to tell Carrie as well. Would you object if we left some of the explanations until Carrie and Christopher are there?'

'No, of course not. Shall we hurry back to the house?'

'Not until I have put one matter right between us.'

'And that is?' Anna tried to sound cool but her heart was beating.

He took her hand. 'There is a fallen tree somewhere, I refuse to go into this argument with us both standing.'

She laughed and they found the tree trunk which Caroline and Anna had occupied and anguished upon so many times. He sat close to her and although he did not attempt to put an arm around her, she was very conscious that their shoulders touched and destroyed the coolness she wished to feel when she was talking to him.

'We must think back to Cherbourg,' he began by saying. 'I was obliged to ask you to marry me, you properly refused; then I tried to explain to you that I would have only a small income and a London house to offer you—'

'You told me that you would be obliged to seek out a wealthy heiress.'

'That is correct.' His words were short.

'And you have found her? That is what you were coming to tell me?' Anna asked the question with a sense of doom.

'No, indeed, it was not—'

But Anna interrupted, risking everything in her next statement.

'I happen to know of a very wealthy young lady whom I think would suit you.'

He tried to read her expression but failed. 'You do? Is she from Somerset?'

'Yes, she is,' was all Anna said.

'I do not suppose that I would know her then. You would have to be kind enough to introduce me.'

'Yes, certainly I will. Would you like me to tell you her name?' Anna felt that she was getting herself deeper and deeper into a deception of her own making.

Philippe was seemingly reluctant. 'I suppose so.'

'It is Miss Anna Starkie.'

He turned fully to face her, gripping her bare arms until she could feel the pain of it.

'Do not jest with me, please.'

'I am quite serious, sir.'

'And your meaning?'

'I am an heiress; I wondered if *I* might suit you.' And as soon as she had said the words, Anna felt ashamed.

He ignored her statement and questioned her harshly. 'You mean that you have money?'

'Yes, I have quite a considerable fortune.'

'How much?'

'Ten thousand pounds.'

'You are roasting me,' he said tersely.

'No, I am serious,' Anna told him. 'My godmother was Lady Joan Hamlyn. She left me a fortune and I did not wish it known. We would have been plagued by gazetted fortune-hunters. Mama agreed, and we put it about that we had inherited a small legacy; we bought ponies for the girls and new gowns and things like that. No one knows the truth except Mama and Christopher.'

'You told Christopher?'

'Yes,' she replied briefly.

'Anna, what can I say?'

Anna took a deep breath as she dared her next words. 'You could say, I love you, I have a good London house and a small pension. And then you could ask me to marry you and we would be quite comfortable.'

'And what would your reply be?' He was still gripping her arms and she thought she could hear a note of unexplained amusement in his voice.

'I would say "Thank you very much, Philippe, I would be pleased to accept".' She glanced at him but he said nothing. 'It would be delightful to have a house in London for the season, and we would easily be able to afford to live at Hatherley Park and make it our country home. It would be very pleasant for us to be near Mama – and presumably to Caroline and Christopher as well.'

He gave a sudden shout of laughter. 'You minx, you rogue, I do believe you mean every word of it.'

'I do, sir. I am not given to falsehoods except when I am persuaded to rescue someone who has been imprisoned by the French ... Philippe, you cannot ... oh, Philippe.' Her voice was drowned for he had taken her roughly into his arms and kissed her almost savagely.

Then he held her away from him and their eyes met, Philippe's seeking her intent, Anna's brimming with laughter.

'You have it all worked out,' he said. 'You not only schemed to get Christopher and Carrie together, you decided that you would like me in your net, as well.'

She grinned. 'That is right. You are so proud that I knew you would never offer for me once you knew that I was possessed of a fortune.'

'And now, Miss Anna Starkie, will you allow me to make my offer in my own way?'

'Yes, of course,' she answered him.

'In the first place, I was called away suddenly from Hatherley Park by a summons from Lord Castlereagh himself. Thora and I talked about it and decided that our charade must end – I will give you the explanation of that when we have Carrie and Christopher with us. Thora decided that she would like to stay in Bath and try for a part at the Theatre Royal – I do not know if she was successful.'

Anna interrupted quickly. 'She is going to play Mrs Malaprop in *The Rivals* which is their next production.'

'Well done Thora,' said Philippe, and continued with his explanation. 'I arrived at the Foreign Office to be told that Lord Castlereagh wanted to see me – he is Foreign Secretary as you will know. Then I discovered that I was to be knighted for my efforts at espionage with Lord Wellington.'

'Philippe, you have been knighted? Oh, I am sure that you deserve it and I offer my sincere congratulations.'

'Thank you, Anna, I will tell you more about it shortly. The main purpose of my meeting with Lord Castlereagh was an offer of a post with Lord Wellington – he is shortly to become the Duke of Wellington as I expect you know – in Paris. You may also know from the newspapers that he is to be ambassador there.'

Anna gazed at him. 'Have you accepted, Philippe?'

He shook his head. 'No, I have not, and I had many reasons. I had spent all those years toiling through Portugal, Spain and France and felt I had seen enough of the continent. But I think the most important thing to me was that I had met the person I wanted to marry, and I wished for a settled life in England with my wife and family. So the Foreign Secretary agreed to it and offered me a pension which was not inconsiderable, and knowing that I had no family seat of my own, he offered to find me a small estate and house.'

'You are going away again, Philippe,' Anna commented feeling a sadness in her heart.

'Wait, Anna, be patient. I knew that the Foreign Office had Hatherley Park at its disposal so I dared to ask for it.'

'You asked for Hatherley Park? Did Lord Castlereagh give it to you?'

'Without hesitation. I have come back to claim it as my own; the lawyers have yet to draw up the deeds, but I am allowed to take up residence immediately.'

Anna was staring at him; she felt very small and foolish and also very cross. 'Do you mean that you let me go on about my fortune and more or less telling you that you could offer for me and have all my money, and you did not need a penny of it?'

His eyes twinkled. 'Yes, that is right. It delighted me.'

Anna became a young tigress. 'Well, it does not delight me. I am ashamed, and it is all your fault.' She beat her hands against his chest and felt tears of anger and mortification trickling down her cheeks. 'You called me a rogue because I said what I did, and it was so forward of me. Now I am ashamed and I never want to see you again.'

She tried to pull away from him but his grasp was too strong. Not only that, he was kissing her. On her cheeks, her lips, her smooth bare shoulders and most audacous of all, she felt his lips tenderly on the soft swell of her breasts which the bodice of her gown did not serve to cover up.

'You cannot, Philippe, you cannot, it is indiscreet,' she stammered, feeling swamped in a tide of emotion and a hot rush of feeling throughout her body.

'It is not indiscreet,' he replied, and paused to kiss her again. 'We are alone in the wood and I love you. I want to show you how much I love you. In fact, now I think of it, I fell in love with you on our very first meeting at this very place.'

'Balderdash,' she managed to say. 'You were at your haughtiest.'

'Maybe I was, but now I will be humble and accept your kind offer of marriage, my dearest Anna.'

'Do not remind me. I blame you entirely for letting me continue when you knew there was no need.'

'Anna, look at me and we will be serious for one little minute.'

She looked up and met loving eyes. 'I love you,' he said quietly, 'and I ask you to be my wife. I did ask you before, but the circumstamces were not right. Please say yes this time.'

Anna gave in. How could she fight with a Philippe in this mood? 'Thank you for your offer, sir, I gladly accept it and I love you very much.'

'Now I can kiss you again.'

'No – well, not for a minute. Are you really Sir Philippe Peverill?'

He smiled and nodded. 'Yes, I am. I was going to tell you about me receiving my knighthood because I was wishing you were there beside me, and Carrie, of course. It is why I was absent for so long and caused you and Carrie such a worry. I had to wait until the Prince of Wales was in London so that he could dub me a knight. And he was so jovial and charming and said he had known my father and he praised me for my work during the war. He was so unlike the tales we hear of him. I was expecting him to be a bloated libertine, but he was quite handsome and very cultured.'

'Oh, I would like to have been there,' Anna said. 'It is a great honour. And do you mean that both of us are now in possession of a fortune? Mine safely in the funds and yours in the acres of Hatherley Park?'

'That is correct, my sweet, your money can be used to keep up Ponderfields and give your sisters a good entry into society. They will not need to wait until they are twenty to make their come-out in Bath as you have done. We could even give them a London season if they would like it and your dear mama could present them at court.'

Anna gazed at him. 'You are not proud and haughty at all,' she told him.

He smiled at her. 'I am proud,' he said. 'I am proud of my promised wife.'

'That is a different meaning,' she argued. 'I thought you very autocratic and proud and that you would never look at us bucolic Starkies.'

'I love my bucolic Starkie,' he said, pulling her close to him. 'She can give me another kiss and then we will hurry to Ponderfields to see what Christopher and Carrie have been up to. We may have some celebrating to do.'

It was somehow not surprising that the two pairs of lovers arrived back at Ponderfields at the same time.

Philippe and Anna had just stepped into the drawing-room to speak to Mrs Starkie when the door was opened again and Caroline and Christopher stood there, both of them with a broad smile.

Caroline's smile became a shriek when she saw Philippe. 'Papa,' she cried out and rushed into his arms. 'Papa, you are home again, I wanted you so badly and, Papa, Christopher has asked me to marry him and I have said yes.'

Christopher joined them speaking quite sternly.

'Caroline, this is no way to behave even if you are excited to see your papa. You know that I must speak with him.'

Caroline looked at him and there was no mistaking the shining love in her eyes. 'I am sorry, Christopher. Can you ask him now?'

'In front of the whole family, Caroline? That is hardly the thing.' Then he addressed himself to Philippe. 'If I might have a few words with you, sir?'

Philippe attempted to be serious. 'We need not go apart, Christopher, I know what you are going to say and the answer is in the affirmative.'

But Christopher insisted that he should put his case properly. 'I must tell you, sir, that I have a very good living at Battiscombe. It includes a beautiful old vicarage which Caroline has seen and likes very much. We do love each other and I would be grateful if you would give me permission to make Caroline an offer.'

Philippe chuckled. 'Shutting the stable door, Christopher? You have already asked Carrie and she has accepted and I am very pleased for you both. I thought from the beginning that you were an admirable young gentleman and it seems I was wrong to link your name with that of Anna. Let us shake hands on the matter and, Carrie, you can give me a kiss, you little moppet. I am very happy for you.'

'Oh, Papa,' sighed Caroline, 'and have you any news for us?' She looked from her father to Anna and could guess what had happened. She laughed with delight. 'While we were playing hide-and-seek in the orchard with the children, Christopher asked me to marry him, and all the time, you had found Anna.' She rushed over to give Anna a hug. 'You are going to marry Papa, I can tell, and you will be my stepmama which is vastly amusing. Do tell us it is true.'

Philippe chided her. 'Calm yourself Carrie, and we will tell you all our news. Yes, I have asked Anna to marry me and I am pleased to say she has accepted me, even though she knows that I am marrying her solely for her fortune . . .'

There was bedlam in the drawing-room.

Anna furiously denied any such thing, Mrs Starkie looked startled, Christopher was not surprised and Caroline spoke the loudest.

'Anna, you do not have a fortune. It was a small legacy, you told me so. And does Papa now need to marry for money? I am sure that you love each other, I have always thought it. Papa, tell us the truth.'

Philippe looked around him and knew that the time had come to make his story plain and to assure them that he was not marrying Anna because of her fortune.

He spoke directly and very kindly to Mrs Starkie 'I must ask your permission to marry your daughter, ma'am. I can assure you that I am very well placed in the world and that Anna's money can be used to keep you comfortably at Ponderfields.' He turned for a moment to Caroline. 'Anna's legacy is a small fortune, my dear, she will tell you all about it. Mrs Starkie, you have three other daughters to bring out and you will be able to have the use of my London house if they would like to come to the capital when the time comes.'

Mrs Starkie could hardly speak and let tears of happiness stream down her cheeks. Philippe kissed her.

'Now, we must all be serious for there are a lot of things I wish you to know; Anna knows some of them already.' He took her hand. 'You tell your family, Anna, it would be immodest of me.'

She gave a chuckle. 'Philippe, we will never think of you as a modest man, but we have cause to be proud of you.' She turned to them all. 'Philippe has been detained in London all this time because he had to await the arrival of the Prince of Wales to confer a knighthood on him. This is in recognition of his services to the government during the Peninsular War; he has also been granted a generous pension, and most important of all, is something which is still partly a mystery to me. It is to do with Hatherley Park, it is now owned by Philippe and we will be setting up our home there—'

'And our nursery,' added a suddenly wicked Philippe.

Everyone in the room laughed with merriment except Anna who confronted Philippe with indignation and pretended horror. 'Philippe, you are not fit to take into society. If I am going to expect that kind of remark from you, I will cry off from our engagement immediately and you can go and find another heiress.'

Philippe bent to kiss her on the cheek. 'I am sorry to put you to shame, my love, you will find that I have a mischievous tongue under my so-called proud exterior. But I promise to be serious now and tell you about Hatherley Park. I have to go back to June of last year and the battle of Vitoria which was a great victory for us and gave us entry into France.' He looked round at them all. 'I don't know if you are interested in the details of the war . . .'

He needed go no further for their was a chorus of eager assent from his audience, and from Christopher in particular as he thought of his brother John.

'It was my practice always to be ahead of the lines to try and gain news of what Soult was going to do next – I always dressed as a French soldier, and I speak the language as a native. Unfortunately, in some way I shall now never discover, they became suspicious of me, and in an argument, I was shot.'

'Philippe!' said a shocked Anna.

'No, do not worry, it was only a flesh wound to the thigh and it has healed. Pierre was always at my side and he succeeded in getting me away. We reached Burgos and sent a dispatch to explain the circumstances. I was ordered back to London, but unfortunately, while we were on the way home, I went down with a fever again. We will never know if it was an infection of the wound, or whether I had picked up typhus or yellow fever. As you all know, it keeps recurring and I have my good Anna to thank for nursing me through it.'

'It was not only me,' said Anna, but she thought she should stay quiet about the Cherbourg incident which she imagined would not be made known to anyone.

Philippe smiled at her. 'I do not forget, Anna,' he said slowly. 'In London, I was told that it was not safe for me to go back for the time being. I was to throw off the suspicious French by acting the part of the English country gentleman. The Foreign Office owned Hatherley Park and I was sent there together with my 'cousin', Thora Peverill, an actress from the London stage.'

He listened to their laughter and chatter. 'Yes, I do know that you have learned about Thora; her performance was impeccable and I can only fault her for not being a good sickroom nurse. But I cannot even complain about that for it brought Anna to me.'

He looked around at Anna and smiled at her.

'I did go back to France from time to time after moving here as you all know; I think that Thora put it about that I was visiting my mistress in Weymouth . . . yes, you can all laugh, she made me out to be a libertine but it did no harm. My base was in Weymouth and that is where Carrie lived with my sister Michelle.

'Now we come to the final part of the story. Lord Castlereagh told me that he would find me an estate to retire to and I had the audacity to ask for Hatherley Park. He willingly agreed and the deeds will soon be drawn up and it will be mine. Anna and I will live there and we will have the joy of being close to you all.'

Philippe turned to Mrs Starkie. 'I think, ma'am, we must have a celebration party. I invite you all including Miss Swinburne with Felicity, Selina and Jane to Hatherley Park tomorrow evening.' Then he turned to Christopher. 'I will welcome you as a son-in-law and on my way back to Hatherley in a moment, I will call at the rectory and invite your mother and father with Jeremy and Matthew. Only John will be missing and we will hope for his speedy return to this country.'

The Boyds and the Starkies together with Caroline, arrived at Hatherley the following evening at the same time; they were all dressed in style.

It somehow did not surprise them to be welcomed by a Mrs Shapter in great distress. 'I don't know what to say I'm sure, Miss Anna. The master has gone off in the carriage with Pierre; very early this morning it were and I'm sure as I don't know where he is. Will you all come in and I will send in some drinks for you in the drawing-room.'

Anna looked at Caroline. 'Do you know what it is all about?' she asked.

Caroline shook her head. 'It is yet another of Papa's mysteries. Surely he cannot have been sent back to France again?'

The whole party made suggestions as to where the new owner of Hatherley Park might be, but somehow not one of them was surprised when the door opened and there stood Philippe. He had a lady on each arm.

'Tante Michelle,' cried out Caroline, and ran laughing into her aunt's arms.

'Oh, it is Thora,' exclaimed Anna with delight as she saw the tall figure of the actress dressed in a gown of gold and white striped satin, with what passed for emeralds around her neck and in her hair. She was smiling radiantly.

And in between them, stood Philippe, from the first to the last the proud Mr and now Sir Philippe Peverill.